REVELATION Of The Lady King

Return of The Crown

Creative Concepts
FOR MINISTRY

ISBN-979-8-9878258-8-4

Editing by: Creative Concepts for Ministry

Front/Back cover by Creative Concepts for Ministry

Photo By: Rich Allela and Dapel Kureng
Photo Model: Sharyl Apond, Kenya Africa (Permission Granted)

Printed and Bound in the USA

First printed January 2018

Revised Print January 2024

Creative Concepts For Ministry
Olive Branch Mississippi
www.creativeconceptsforministry.com

Ordering information:

Exclusive discounts are available on quantity purchases by corporations, associations, educators, and others. For details, contact the publisher at the above-listed address.

U.S. trade bookstores and wholesalers: Please contact
Creative Concepts For Ministry

Website: www.creativeconceptforministry.com

Email: creativeconcepts4ministry@gmail.com

Dedication

"This book is dedicated to my mother, Mattie Goods. You are forever my Lady King. Rest in peace, Momma. To my daughters, Laquanda, Yalonda, and Demetrice, may you always know your worth. And finally, to the woman holding this book today, may you embrace your kingship."

Table of Content

From The Author

This book is an intentional and sacred work, given by divine inspiration. I have written it under the full guidance of the Holy Spirit, with the earnest intention to stir the hearts of God's daughters. I have carefully woven historical and biblical facts about our journey through time within these pages. Throughout each page, I have endeavored to call attention to the resilience, bravery, boldness, and authority that we embody.

Within theses pages, I have been careful not to omit our functionality and how it differs from our male counterparts. Yet, I felt obliged to speak of our inclusion, our freedom, our strength, and our validation that comes solely from God. As I have written, I have hoped, and even envisioned us standing once again in the face of our Adam, reclaiming our equality, and embracing our purpose as his 'ezer kenegdo' - a suitable companion, flesh of his flesh and bone of His bone, worthy to rule alongside Him.

I am God's Daughter, and a masterpiece, I AM.

"For reasons we have yet to embark upon, someone decided that being a girl did not make for a good king. —I am here to prove them wrong."

—Connie Dotson

And because you are sons, God has sent forth the Spirit of His Son into your hearts, crying out, 'Abba, Father!' Therefore you are no longer a slave but a son, and if a son, then an heir of God through Christ.—Galatians 4:6-7

"MY MOUTH WILL NOT REMAIN SILENT ABOUT OUR PLIGHT. NOR WILL I RETREAT IN THE FACE OF ADVERSITY.
—Connie Dotson

Definition of a Lady King

The term "Lady King" is a divine inspiration from the Holy Spirit, signifying a proclamation of women's return to their pre-fall position. "Lady" represents her God-given role as a woman, emphasizing her unique capacity as the one with a womb. "King" reconnects her to her rightful place of authority and dominion in the earthly realm, as outlined in Genesis 1:26-27. It defines her identity before the fall. This revelation of the "Lady King" serves as a clarion call for women everywhere to arise and reclaim their identity as kings and priests in the earthly realm. It symbolizes the breaking of the curse.

—*Lady Kings Arise!*

Proclamation

Lady Kings Arise!

Awaken, Lady Kings! Rise from your slumber and fully embrace your true identity. Break free from the chains of bondage, guilt, and shame that have long obscured your truth. Liberate yourselves from the confines of destitution and wholeheartedly accept this revelation of your freedom. Stir, shift, and shake off your constraints. Raise your head high and stand with resilience. I call to you from the farthest corners of the earth. Your journey has been difficult, but the time for your restoration is now. Daughters, know that you are not forgotten; you are God's daughters. As His daughters, you are rightful heirs to a royal throne, and as heirs, you are indeed Kings.

– Let us return to Eden to reclaim and celebrate this truth.

Revelation

Revelation, from a biblical perspective, is the act by which God discloses Himself or communicates His will to humanity. This divine unveiling comes in various forms and encompasses both the revealing of God's character and His purposes. It is fundamentally about God making known the unseen—His nature, His plans, His commands, and His promises—to mankind.

How long will this generation of people mourn over the gender of the king, go, and anoint my daughters, for this is the hour that their mantles shall be restored."

Model: Sharyl Apond, Kenya Africa

Photo Credit: **Rich Allela** and **Dapel Kureng**

Introduction

It is the spirit that quickeneth; the flesh profiteth nothing: the words that I speak unto you, they are spirit, and they are life. —John 6:63 (KJV)

After spending hours in intense prayer, I believed I had received the message I was meant to share. I was scheduled to speak at a women's prayer retreat, and I had selected a message from the *My Circle My Life Manual*, a topic I had been teaching successfully for months. But with just a few hours left before heading to the retreat, a strong urge led me back to prayer.

Suddenly, the Holy Spirit spoke a completely different message. His words were unfamiliar and not based on logic or reasoning. I had never heard anything like it before. He instructed me to tell the women that they were not just ladies but also kings. He declared that He had restored their kingship and called them to the frontline for the advancement of God's Kingdom on earth. He reminded me of the anointing of David as king of Israel (Samuel 16:1-7) and compared it to today's Daughters of Zion. He said, *"How long will this generation mourn over the gender of the king? Go and anoint my daughters, for this is the hour their mantles are restored."*

This revelation was entirely contrary to what I had previously been taught. It challenged my confidence in delivering a message that so profoundly contradicted my cultural beliefs and understanding.

When expounding on a deep revelation, it's important to remember that we shouldn't rely solely on our intellect to get the message across. When we do, we miss out on the treasures of the King's heart. Our sermons end up being based on human doctrine rather than God's divine laws (Matthew 15:9), making our messages more informative than effective.

For this reason, the Rhema word from God seems foreign to many. Therefore, many of God's people are not open to new utterances from God. With this in mind, I understood that the message of the lady king was no small feat. I would have to fiercely push through the opposition of many to release this message. However, I am confident that through prayer and the guidance of the Holy Spirit, many will receive this revelation and find healing and deliverance.

I am not a Bible scholar. I certainly don't possess a wall of degrees to validate myself. However, my Father in heaven has trusted me with this revelation of the lady king. He sanctions these words. He has permitted me to write them on these pages. Wherever they shall go will be at His command, and the lives that they shall touch will be at His discretion.

If you are reading this book, God's message is simple—you are a king! You are an equal companion suitable for your male counterpart. Therefore, you have the liberty to act and respond as a king in every situation. You are not inferior to anyone. You are a helper not just to the male gender but to humanity. Your assignment on the earth is different, but your authority and ability to have dominion are equal.

This message of the lady king contradicts societal and cultural norms. It directly opposes such beliefs as male superiority and women being the subservient gender. It refocuses our attention on the woman in her pre-fall condition by differentiating functionality from superiority. It inspires women to recover their God-given mantle or original identity. It is a clarion call to interrupt the destructive patterns created toward women due to a distorted image. This journey of discovery guides all women in pursuit of their rightful crown. Eventually, it places each woman back in the face of her Adam so that he, too, may rediscover her true identity and the immeasurable value she possesses and bestows upon him.

Women are often encouraged to function beneath the veil of false submission, which in many cases is only a cunning means of dictatorship. In chapter six, *"The Truth about Submission,"* we will discuss the idea of submission and how God intended for it to be embraced. We will address its relevance to the crowning of her Lady King and hopefully put to rest some misconceptions of what it means to submit.

Women are often found waiting to be recognized or validated in many areas of ministry. Many have spent years holding on to visions and dreams waiting to be confirmed by a man. While they are waiting, visions and dreams burn violently within. Subtle disapproval and open lack of support imply that women are not qualified to lead without male figures. And without a revelation of identity, many will die without ever living out their life's purpose.

Women build a vast majority of ministries. They devote themselves to work under tyrant male leaders and are encouraged to remain silent while their gifts and callings are plundered and prostituted. We have used and allowed our bodies to be used as an offering in exchange for high places.

We have nursed and uplifted visions that belonged to another person. We have worked behind the scenes and refused to take credit for our contributions—often being told that our dreams and visions must take a back seat.

Even in this generation, women have not received the accolades they deserve. Many have operated by blind faith and have been subject to the mastery of the pulpits. In most cases, we have not been offered a single thank you for being the driving force behind another man's vision. However, God is saying, "Come forth, my Lady Kings. He will validate you and release you to launch forward in your purpose."

"And he took the damsel by the hand, and said unto her, Talitha cumi; which is, being interpreted, Damsel, I say unto thee, arise." - Mark 5:41 (KJV)

I have been given a steady hand to write this revelation of our identity. I plead with you to take notice of this truth. Those days of old must diminish at the dawning of this new day and we must shift into a new paradigm. The real Lady Kings must arise from the shadows of defeat. We must emerge from the deep shadows of oppression and our rightful place.

We must be mindful of hearing and embracing this message; the move of God that is about to take place in the earthly realm will involve you. Our dormant posture cannot usher in this new movement. And being ignorant of our identity will not stop the enemy's attacks. Therefore, by the time you finish reading this book, God will no longer offer grace for those excuses we give for not walking in our purpose. Because truth is your freedom, you will be held accountable for how you respond once you have tasted it.

As you turn the pages of this book, deliverance and healing will happen. Then boldness and tenacity to fight the good fight will come. As you embrace the truth throughout each page, dreams and visions will be reborn, and you will discover the king inside you.

Highlights of A Lady King

Harriet Beecher Stowe

Author and Abolitionist | (1811-1896)

The longest way must have its close - the gloomiest night will wear on to a morning."—Uncle Tom's Cabin, Harriet Beecher Stowe. 1852

Harriet Beecher Stowe was a remarkable American author and abolitionist. She is best known for her groundbreaking novel, "Uncle Tom's Cabin," which was published in 1852. Born into a prominent and devoutly religious family, Stowe was deeply influenced by her upbringing and the strong moral values instilled in her.

Uncle Tom's Cabin[1]" was a literary masterpiece that vividly portrayed the harsh realities of slavery in the United States. The novel follows the lives of enslaved African Americans and depicts the brutality they endured under the institution of slavery. It showcased the inhumanity of the system, the separation of families, and the struggles for freedom.

What made Stowe's work truly groundbreaking was its emotional impact. Her words struck a chord with readers across the nation, evoking strong emotions and stirring the conscience of many. It is said that when President Abraham Lincoln met Harriet Beecher Stowe during the Civil War, he remarked, "So you're the little woman who wrote the book that started this great war.

[1] Uncle Tom's Cabinet:1852|Literary work by Harriet Beecher Stowe can be purchase on amazon.

Stowe's novel ignited a fierce movement against slavery, contributing significantly to the growing anti-slavery sentiment in the North. It inspired countless individuals to take action, join the abolitionist cause, and demand an end to the institution of slavery. Her powerful words and storytelling played a pivotal role in the eventual emancipation of enslaved African Americans.

Biblical Example

Deborah

Prophetess and Judge of Israel | Judges Chapter 4-5

"Very well," Deborah said, "I will go with you. But because of the way you are going about this, the honor will not be yours, for the Lord will hand Sisera over to a woman."—Judges 4-9

Deborah, a pivotal figure in the Bible, is prominently featured in the Book of Judges (Chapters 4 and 5). Her story is significant for several reasons, notably because she was both a prophetess and the only female judge among the twelve judges of ancient Israel. *Her unique role in Israel's history showcases her as a leader of great faith, wisdom, and courage.*

Deborah's role as a prophetess and judge is unique in the biblical narrative. Judges 4:4 explicitly states, "Deborah, a prophetess, the wife of Lappidoth, was leading Israel at that time." This dual role endowed her with spiritual authority to deliver God's messages and judicial power to govern the people of Israel.

During Deborah's time, the Israelites were oppressed by Jabin, the king of Canaan, and his commander Sisera. The biblical account describes the Israelites' suffering under Jabin's harsh rule for twenty years, which led them to cry out to the Lord for deliverance.

The Call to Barak: In Judges 4:6-7, Deborah summons Barak, a military leader, and instructs him on God's behalf to gather an army to fight against Sisera's forces. Notably, she prophesies that the honor of defeating Sisera would go to a woman, which was unusual in the context of ancient Near Eastern culture.

Deborah's faith and leadership were instrumental in the battle against the Canaanites. She accompanied Barak to Mount Tabor, where they faced Sisera's formidable army. Despite their inferior military strength, Deborah's faith in God's promise led Israel to a miraculous victory.

Judges Chapter 5, known as "The Song of Deborah," is a victory hymn that Deborah and Barak sing to celebrate their triumph. This song is one of the oldest extant pieces of Hebrew poetry and offers insights into early Israelite culture and religion. It praises the Lord for the victory and recounts the heroic acts of various tribes and individuals, including Jael, who ultimately kills Sisera.

Deborah stands out not only as a leader in a male-dominated society but also as a spiritual guide who trusted in God's power and guidance. Her story is often cited as an example of strong female leadership in the Bible, and it challenges traditional gender roles in leadership and warfare.

Deborah's story is a testament to the multifaceted roles women played in biblical history and remains an inspiration for leadership, faith, and courage across various religious and cultural contexts. *Her legacy continues to be celebrated and studied for its profound impact on biblical* history and its inspirational role in encouraging equal and diverse leadership roles in various spheres of life.[2]

[2] The biblical account of Deborah can be found in Judges' chapters four through five.

The answer had finally come to me. The person or persons I was waiting for validation from did not exist in human form. This single revelation removed the tug-of-war that had flooded my mind since I first understood my salvation and my call to ministry.

—I Am a Lady But I am A King Too!

Picture Credit: **Rich Allela** and **Dapel Kureng**

Chapter 01
The Anchoring of My Mind

Be anxious for nothing, but in everything by prayer and supplication, with thanksgiving, let your requests be made known to God; and the peace of God, which surpasses all understanding, will guard your hearts and minds through Christ Jesus.
-Philippians 4:6-7 (NKJV)

The validation I had so desperately hoped for was hidden in plain sight. Although obscured by religion and tradition, it was tucked away neatly in God's Word. Destiny beckoned to me. Yet, my ability to reach for it was imprisoned by the fear of failure, coupled with years of yearning for affirmation from others. My dreams and visions had found a quiet refuge in the sanctuary of my mind.

At times, I hesitated to put them on paper, instead waiting for a distinguished pastor or spiritual leader to mentor me. I had embraced the notion that one must submit to a spiritual father and await their recognition and validation before taking any steps toward the mandate or the call that God had given me.

For many years, I surrendered every dream and vision to another person, fervently praying for their affirmation and permission to embark on my ministry journey. In my mind's eye, I envisioned myself sitting at my pastor's feet, eagerly soaking in the wisdom and guidance needed to fulfill the call on my life.

I made sure to conform, both in appearance and speech, to match those around me. I vowed to be an exemplary student and a devoted daughter. Yet, despite all those years of submission under the covering of a spiritual leader, the validation I yearned for never arrived. I remained in a state of suspension, but my heart was filled with vision.

Understanding this revelation nullifies the war against our identity and places our enemy at a disadvantage when warring against us. When we truly embrace our God-given identity, we will not need to explain who we are or try to justify the call, assignment, or ministry appointment God has placed upon us.

Similarly, I considered my marriage and the desire for my husband to join me in ministry. I made every effort to persuade him to take the initiative in embracing the vision that was welling up inside me. After all, I had been taught that a good wife should wait for her husband to lead and follow him in every endeavor. Consequently, I disregarded that small voice inside me urging me to move forward—I surrendered to the wait.

I was waiting, at least until my husband got on board. However, there was one significant challenge. I had been a Christian for 20 years, whereas my husband had only a few years of experience in his faith. His understanding of spiritual matters was still evolving, and he wasn't as attuned to the things of God. Influenced by societal norms about collaborative ministry roles for couples, he lacked a clear roadmap to guide us both into this new destiny.

I reasoned that in this aspect of our marriage, I should take the lead. Nevertheless, I felt compelled to adhere to the belief that I should unconditionally submit to my husband's leadership in every situation.

This scenario highlighted an important lesson I learned and wish to share with you: Discovering your identity in Christ doesn't always align seamlessly with traditional expectations. Therefore, we must exercise patience, allowing our loved ones the necessary time to comprehend and embrace our freedom in Christ—it's a journey of mutual growth and understanding.

Nonetheless, we must embrace this truth, even in the face of others' reluctance. This truth grants us the freedom to accept our purpose. I believe that living our purpose as God predetermined, being and doing precisely what God has called us to, is the highest honor we can bestow upon our Creator.

Finally, God Anchored My Mind

The answer had finally come to me. The person or persons I was waiting for validation from did not exist in human form. This single revelation removed the tug-of-war that had flooded my mind since I first understood my salvation and my call to ministry. Suddenly, like an anchored ship, the conflict in my mind had ended. And my mind was made sturdy in the truth of this revelation—I am a Lady, but I am King Too!

This profound revelation extended beyond just my personal experience; it encompassed the numerous misguided perceptions that have accumulated over time for women across the globe. Like many of these women, I found myself firmly entrenched in a stance I labeled "WAIT." While this position permitted me to dream, it simultaneously held me captive to a constant need for external validation. Consequently, many of my God-ordained visions and dreams lay dormant. However, the Holy Spirit began to unravel these misconceptions, granting me the liberty not only to dream and envision but also to fully embrace and possess all that God has purposefully intended for me.

He directed my focus towards extraordinary women who have paved the way throughout history. I reflected on remarkable figures like Sojourner Truth, Harriet Tubman, Maya Angelou, Oprah Winfrey, and Hillary Clinton, among others. Did these women wait for someone else to propel them into action? Did they spend years on hold, awaiting a single word from a man to ignite their spirits? Did they ever regard their womanhood as a pretext for enslavement — not the physical kind, but the kind that seizes the mind and stifles dreams?

It's clear that extraordinary women cannot be contained or defined by tradition or religion. They are meant to be different, to challenge the world and lead us toward the path of truth that's laid out by heaven. These women are destined to leave a legacy behind.

When they discover the truth, they run with it and refuse to accept 'no' as an answer. Every challenge propels them toward remarkable victories. Their names are etched in the annals of history, inspiring generations of young girls to dream beyond their immediate surroundings. These women carry a burning fire within them and represent what a Lady King should look like on earth today.

The Battle isn't Over!

When a woman discovers who she truly is, her life is profoundly changed. She no longer walks in the shadows of inferiority. Inherently she's able to move into a new dimension of her anointing and birth dreams and vision that significantly advances the Kingdom of God on earth. However, history teaches us that the reclamation of a stolen identity often invites warfare. Nonetheless, once we discover our identity, we must secure it in our hearts and anchor our minds in its principles, refusing to exist or operate in any other way.

We should also prepare to stand against anything that opposes this truth. It will mean rejecting tradition, defying religious constraints, and wholeheartedly embracing dominion and authority in the face of adversity. Before continuing this journey, we must reflect and ask ourselves: Are we ready? Are we prepared to receive the crown? This is no small feat, but we can face opposition with the assurance of our guaranteed victory through God's promises. If you stick with me through the pages of this journey we will arrive in front of your crown—however, it will be up to you to receive it.

While women have made significant strides, the battle isn't over. Our past struggles have molded us and prepared us for future victories. With that in mind, I share this message with the women of my generation to restore a mantle that has been unjustly distorted. It's a mantle of strength and courage, a bold declaration of our kingship.

The Revelation of The Lady King, challenges us to move beyond the confines of religion and tradition, encouraging us to seek God's voice for the truth about our identity. It urges us to pursue wisdom from God for a genuine interpretation of His Word. Through this journey, we can finally understand the vast authority, power, and dominion that God has bestowed upon His daughters.

I'm fully aware that this revelation may raise eyebrows, perhaps even be met with resistance. Some may use scripture to challenge it, but my mind is anchored in this truth. I am equipped with answers to address misconceptions and misinterpretations of God's Word regarding women. Although challenging, it's an honor to be one of the many vessels chosen by God to speak to the women of this generation.

"May our hearts be ready for the challenges we will face as we plunge forward in this truth. My dear sisters, anchor your mind, and let's fight to re-discover our identity."

Highlights of A Lady King

01: The Anchoring of My Mind | Malala Yousafzai Advocate Education for Girls (July 1997)

Malala Yousafzai is a living testament to the power of education and the resilience of the human spirit. Born on July 12, 1997, in Mingora, Pakistan, Malala grew up in a region where the importance of education was often overshadowed by political turmoil and gender discrimination. However, her father, Ziauddin Yousafzai, was a vocal advocate for education and instilled in Malala the belief that every girl had the right to learn.

Malala's life took a drastic turn in 2009 when the Taliban gained control of the Swat Valley, where she lived. Under the Taliban's oppressive rule, girls were banned from attending school, and their rights were severely restricted. Malala, even at a young age, refused to be silenced. She began to anonymously blog for the BBC Urdu, detailing her experiences and her unwavering commitment to education.

As Malala's prominence grew, so did the danger to her life. On October 9, 2012, as she was riding a bus home from school, a masked gunman boarded the bus and asked for her by name. He then shot her in the head, leaving her in critical condition. Malala's miraculous survival became a global symbol of courage and resistance.

Malala was airlifted to Birmingham, England, for medical treatment and rehabilitation. Her story garnered worldwide attention, and she used her newfound platform to advocate for girls' education on an international scale. She co-authored the memoir "I Am Malala: The Girl Who Stood Up for Education and Was Shot by the Taliban," which further amplified her message.

In 2014, at the age of 17, Malala became the youngest-ever recipient of the Nobel Peace Prize for her advocacy of girls' right to an education. This prestigious award solidified her as a global symbol of hope and change.

Malala's journey embodies the theme of "The Anchoring of My Mind." Despite facing life-threatening adversity, she remained steadfast in her belief in the power of education to transform lives. Her unwavering commitment to education has inspired millions around the world, demonstrating that a determined mind can overcome even the darkest of circumstances.

Malala Yousafzai's fight for girls' education reflects the importance of education and the power of the mind. Her story serves as a reminder that the pursuit of knowledge can anchor one's mind and spirit, enabling them to overcome the greatest challenges and make a profound impact on the world.[3]

---

[3] See cite page # for data reference see reference page 189

Biblical Example

Huldah

Prohetess 2 Kings 22:14-20

Huldah is another significant female figure in the Hebrew Bible, known for her role as a prophetess during the reign of King Josiah of Judah. Her story, though brief, is significant for its portrayal of a woman's authoritative role in religious and national matters in ancient Israel. Huldah's account is primarily found in 2 Kings 22:14-20.

Huldah's Prophetic Role: Huldah is introduced in 2 Kings 22:14 as a prophetess residing in Jerusalem. This introduction establishes her as a recognized spiritual authority in the city.

Consultation by King Josiah's Officials: King Josiah's officials, including the high priest Hilkiah, sought Huldah's counsel after the discovery of a book of the law during the renovation of the Temple. This event is detailed in 2 Kings 22:14, where it says, "So Hilkiah the priest, Ahikam, Achbor, Shaphan, and Asaiah went to Huldah the prophetess."

Huldah's Prophecy: In 2 Kings 22:15-17, Huldah delivers a prophecy concerning Judah's future. She prophesies disaster for the kingdom because of the people's disobedience to the words of the book, stating that God's wrath has been kindled against them.

Message of Hope to Josiah: Interestingly, in 2 Kings 22:18-20, Huldah also conveys a message of hope specifically to King Josiah. She acknowledges

Josiah's humility and responsiveness to the words of the book, and as a result, she prophesies that the disaster she foretold would not occur during his reign.

Legacy and Significance: Huldah's story is significant for several reasons. Firstly, her role as a prophetess who is consulted by the king's officials highlights the respect and authority, she held in a male-dominated society. Secondly, her prophecy played a crucial role in Josiah's religious reforms, which are extensively documented in the biblical narrative.

Huldah's presence in the biblical text, though brief, underscores the impact and importance of female prophetic voices in the religious and cultural life of ancient Israel. Her story reflects the significant, yet often understated roles women played in the shaping of Israelite religion and society.[4]

[4] The story of Huldah can be found in 2 Kings 22:14:20.

Power Dominion and authority are God's original declaration about humanity, and it bears no gender specifics. Likewise, God didn't create Adam as superior to Eve.

Photo Credit: **Rich Allela** and **Dapel Kureng**

Chapter 02

The Revelation of Inclusion

"'In the last days, God says, I will pour out my Spirit on all people. Your sons and daughters will prophesy, your young men will see visions, your old men will dream dreams. —1 Corinthians 2:14 (NKJV)

The Holy Spirit is gentle. I am amazed by His guidance and consistent love through this work. Through these pages, He guides us to a place of restoration and healing that is simply amazing. Heavenly Father desires that you know that He did not leave you out. Although history has painted a picture lavished with tales of exclusion for women, God has applied the healing salve of grace and redemption and unveiled the revelation of our inclusion.

It is a common misunderstanding amongst believers that God created Adam, and because Adam was lonely, He created Eve to fill in the blank. This idea suggests that the woman was an afterthought whose only purpose was to satisfy the male gender. However, our God is all-knowing (Psalms 139). He knows the beginning and ending before it comes to fruition. Because of this, He sets plans in motion for humanity according to what is ahead. He holds times and seasons in His hand and disburses eternal benefits within its frame. Understanding this attribute of God will help us comprehend the creation of woman and perhaps breathe a fresh revelation about the essence of our existence.

First and Foremost

Humanity is God's greatest masterpiece on earth. The Bible unfolds the events as God created His beloved humans. The story is beautiful and shares with us the intentions and mindset of the Father when He created mankind.

"For we are God's masterpiece. He has created us anew in Christ Jesus, so we can do the good things he planned for us long ago." - Ephesians 2:10 (NLT)

However, it is also complex and challenging to understand by the carnal mind alone (1 Cor 2:14). It speaks of gender specifics, dominion, and power. It combines both males and females yet alludes to one man (Genesis 5:2). Then it separates the pair and declares they will become one again (Genesis 2:22). It leads us through a dimension of creation that scientists cannot truly explain because the mystery of creation is only understood by the guidance of the Holy Spirit.

Grasping the heart of the Father, His attributes, and His character, deepens our understanding of creation's message. Viewing creation from the perspective of our Father's heart unveils the story of our inclusion, affirming that God's original design never intended for one human being to dominate another. Nor did He overlook His daughters. His love for us was intricately woven into the fabric of creation from the very beginning of time.

A Closer Look

In the average institutional church, it is almost heresy for women and men to have equal authority. However, a closer look at Genesis reveals a truth that has been dormant for ages.

> *"And God said, Let us make man in our image, after our likeness: and let them have dominion over the fish of the sea, and over the fowl of the air, and over the cattle, and over all the earth, and over every creeping thing that creepeth upon the earth. So, God created man in his own image, in the image of God created he him; male and female created he them." - Genesis 1:26-27 (KJV)*

The above scripture speaks a profound truth that all women are encouraged to embrace. Within these verses, we find the clear will of the Father for His daughters—that, akin to our male counterparts, we too were created in God's image. Consequently, we possess the authority to rule and conquer the earth. This undeniable truth should serve as our steadfast defense whenever our identity is questioned or challenged.

If we look at these scriptures through unveiled eyes, we will discover that it was not the plan of God to make us unsafe in an environment that He created for us. Neither did He intend for His daughters to live a life subservient to the male gender or be forced into [5]legalistic slavery. To truly walk in the truth about our identity, we must challenge and dismantle the misconceptions that oppose God's word concerning our identity and roles.

---

[5] Legalistic slavery is a condition where individuals rigidly adhere to religious laws or norms, often sacrificing personal freedom and joy, leading to feelings of guilt and spiritual exhaustion.

Indeed, embarking on such a journey to realize a world where men and women share equal authority can be both daunting and profoundly rewarding, especially as many have yet to even imagine such a possibility.

> Understanding this revelation nullifies the war against our identity and places our enemy at a disadvantage when warring against us. When we truly embrace our God-given identity, we will not need to explain who we are or try to justify the call, assignment, or ministry appointment God has placed upon us.

It is my prayer that women across the globe will come to accept God's plans for them and, possibly, reclaim the entirety of their God-bestowed identity. The truth awaits us, ready to be embraced. Yet, to uncover it, we must rid our minds of traditionalism, legalism, and cultural norms. Perhaps in doing so, we will arrive at an untainted truth about God's intention for His daughters!

A Part of The Original Plan

From the beginning of Genesis, the story of God's creation unfolds. We see an omnipotent God speaking and calling things into existence (Genesis 1:1-24). He decrees and declares, and it is done. Even in its imaginary form, it is beautiful to behold. With each new addition to His creation, God would declare that it was good (Genesis 1:4, 10, 12, 18, 21, 25, 31), suggesting that it meets the standard for which He created it.

Whenever someone sets out to create something, they usually know its purpose before starting. Therefore, it is safe to assume God was preparing a place for His masterpiece—humanity. He had a purpose in mind for the vast creation that He created. That purpose was to place humanity in its midst and give them power and dominion over His creation.

"The heaven, even the heavens, are the Lord's; but the earth He has given to the children of men." – Psalms 115:16 (NKJV)

Dominion & Authority

After God created the earth and everything therein, He revealed His intentions for the completed work. He proclaimed, "Let us make man in our own image and let THEM have dominion over every living thing that creeps upon the face of the earth" (Genesis 1:26-27). The use of "Them" being plural refers to humanity as a whole, underscoring that God intended for both males and females to exercise dominion and authority—over the earthly realm.

Dominion and authority are God's original declaration about humanity, and they bear no gender specifics. Likewise, God didn't create Adam as superior to Eve, which we will discuss later in this chapter.

Before moving forward, it's crucial that we understand the significance of fully embracing both dominion and authority. Many of us grasp the concept of dominion—we know that as God's creation, we are called to rule the earth. Yet, as women, our visions and dreams often come to a standstill. We hear the call of God; we recognize what we are capable of, but we find ourselves waiting for permission to obey Him. This hesitancy stems partly from treating dominion and authority as two separate ideas. Historically, we've been taught to believe that women are meant to operate under the guidance and control of a male figure. However, the divine order of authority is not gender-specific. Since the dawning of the resurrected Christ, women have been liberated from the constraints of the fall. To truly embrace freedom, we must reclaim the authority that has been restored to us.

Let's delve deeper into the broader meanings of both dominion and authority, understanding them not as separate forces but as complementary elements of our calling.

In the context of Genesis 1:26-27, the terms "dominion" and "authority" share similarities but bear distinct nuances. "Dominion" denotes sovereignty, control, and the power to govern creation, highlighting a hierarchical relationship between humanity and other life forms on Earth. It advocates for an active engagement in stewardship and governance, signaling not only the capacity to rule but also the obligation to wisely manage and safeguard Earth's resources.

Conversely, "authority" signifies the right or power to issue commands, make decisions, and ensure compliance. It represents a more expansive term that might include the notion of dominion but primarily accentuates the legitimacy and entitlement to wield power.

In this scriptural context, while "dominion" particularly emphasizes our role as custodians with authority over creation, *"authority" underscores the endowed power and right to enact this role.* Although the terms may be used interchangeably in some contexts, "dominion" within Genesis underscores a deeper layer of responsibility and stewardship. While authority gives us the right to exercise that stewardship.

This is the pivotal moment in which we, as daughters of God, must fully understand our role! It's essential for us to come into the knowledge, understanding, and acceptance of our authority on Earth. Without this comprehension, we risk remaining in a position of subservience, perpetually constrained, and ultimately, we may spend our lives waiting for a male figure to validate us. However, my dear lady king, the time has come for you to empower yourself. It's time to give yourself permission to shine bright like a diamond. Embrace your God-given authority and step into the light with confidence and determination, breaking free from the shadows of waiting and expectation. Let your brilliance light up the path not just for yourself, but for others who look to you for inspiration and leadership.

Correcting Myths & Misinterpretations

Understanding this revelation nullifies the war against our identity and places our enemy at a disadvantage when warring against us. When we truly embrace our God-given identity, we will not need to explain who we are or try to justify the call, assignment, or ministry appointment God has placed upon us. God already declared through His infinite truth—His daughters are and have always been a part of His plan.

"For in Christ Jesus, you are all sons of God, through faith. For as many of you as were baptized into Christ have put on Christ. There is neither Jew nor Greek, there is neither slave nor free, there is no male and female, for you are all one in Christ Jesus. And if you are Christ's, then you are Abraham's offspring, heirs according to promise." – Galatians 3: 26-29

It may seem elementary to explain this revelation of inclusion to any mature believer. It may even sound like blasphemy to those who have not ventured beyond religiosity and manufactured doctrine. The real trick of the enemy is to keep us blind to the revelation of who we are. After all, what better way to control a man/woman than to strip them of their identity?

Genesis 1:26-27 should release a great yearning within women everywhere to return to our identity. It should empower us to shake off the residue of guilt and shame that accompanied the fall. *Because through this scripture, God reveals His very desire for* humanity when He said, "Let us make man in our image and let THEM have dominion..." *According to Webster's dictionary, the word "THEM" is plural and means more than one.* Hence the understanding that God wasn't speaking exclusively to the male gender. The scripture implies that God fully intended for both males and females to have dominion and authority in the earth.

Because man and woman were created in God's image, they were both given authority in the earthly realm. If this was our actual state before the fall, then the fall interrupted God's divine order and marred the original condition of creation.

Some scriptures have been taken out of context to prove that women are inferior to the male gender and should always be subordinate to them. The following scriptures are examples of such interpretations.

"I do not permit a woman to teach or to assume authority over a man; she must be quiet. For Adam was formed first, then Eve. And Adam was not the one deceived; it was the woman who was deceived and became a sinner." - 1 Timothy 2:12-14 (NIV)

"Women should remain silent in the churches. They are not allowed to speak, but must be in submission, as the law says. If they want to inquire about something, they should ask their own husbands at home; for it is disgraceful for a woman to speak in the church."—1 Corinthians 14:34-35 (NIV)

These scriptures are the basis by which many well-meaning ministries forbid women to preach, teach, or prophesy in church. However, in 1

Corinthians 11:5, The Apostle Paul instructs women about how to present themselves when they pray and prophesy in the church.

> *"But every woman who prays or prophesies with her head uncovered dishonors her head—it is the same as having her head shaved." – 1 Corinthians 11:5*

For this reason alone, we cannot take this scripture to mean God did not want women to speak in the Church.

We cannot deny that these scriptures exist or that one of our most beloved apostles wrote them. Therefore, we must confront them head-on. Understanding these scriptures will help us debunk misguided interpretations and dismantle strongholds that enter by lack of knowledge and religious agendas created to keep women silent or, as some say, "in their rightful place."

There are many different interpretations of 1 Timothy 2:11-12; however, we can only accept those considering the entire counsel of God's word. If not, we call God unstable or contradictory. And we know that God's word is infinite—all of heaven and earth shall pass away but His word will stand forever as a guiding light for His creation. (Matthew 24:35)

Let's consider a couple of things about those scriptures. First, I want to point out something essential in unraveling the meaning and tone of scripture. Scripture must be studied, understood, and validated by other scriptures. It is detrimental that we present God's word accurately, fearing even the idea of misrepresenting or misinterpreting His message.

Because the ancient bible was written in Hebrew, Aramaic, and Greek and translated into different languages, some word definitions are lost in translation[6]. For this reason, we must study scripture closely to present correct biblical doctrine. We should never present as doctrinal truth our ideologies nor base doctrine on our traditions. It is important to note that many years of practicing something don't make it right. Moving forward, we will use scripture to discover the meaning and intent of the apostle's instructions. And perhaps put to rest the myth that women hold less authority than men.

God Approves Women in Leadership

First, let's make a few discoveries about God's woman. If we stroll through scripture, we will find that women ruled in power and demonstration throughout the Old and New Testaments. They were a significant part of biblical history and were used mightily by God. Let's consider a few of these powerful women from the Old Testament and New Testament. (Genesis 21:1-3)

Sarah, the wife of Abraham, stands as a remarkable figure in biblical history, used extraordinarily by God. Despite her advanced age, Sarah was blessed to give birth to Isaac at the age of 90, who would go on to become one of the founding patriarchs of Israel. Her story is a powerful testament to faith, patience, and the fulfillment of God's promises, even when they seem impossible by human standards.

Miriam the Prophetess holds a significant place as Moses's sister and a key figure in the Exodus story. She vigilantly watched over Moses when he was placed in the Nile River, ensuring his safety and even arranging

[6] Bible Blender. (2019). The complete history of Bible translations – how the Word was delivered from God to our modern-day bibles. Retrieved from https://www.bibleblender.com;

for their own mother to nurse and care for him, as described in Exodus 1:22—2:4. Miriam's role expanded significantly as she later emerged as a leader alongside Moses during the exodus of Israel from 400 years of slavery. Notably, after crossing the Red Sea, Miriam led the women in prophetic worship and dance, celebrating their miraculous escape and freedom (Exodus 15:20-21). Recognized and sent by God, Miriam was chosen to assist Moses in leading the Israelites, underscoring her pivotal role and divine appointment as outlined in Micah 6:4.

***Deborah The Judge*:** Deborah was a judge of Israel; Israel came to her to judge matters of importance. She was also a prophet and a woman of war. She prophesied to Barak that God would give him victory over the Jablin's army. Barak feared Jablin's mighty army and declared he would not go to war without Deborah. She prophesied that Jablin himself would fall at the hands of a woman. That prophecy was fulfilled in Judges 4:21-22. Deborah remained judge over Israel for 40 years, and from this triumphant victory, the land had peace.

Mary Magdalene: Mary stands out as a pivotal figure in the New Testament, showcasing the profound role women played in the early Christian movement. A devoted follower of Jesus, Mary Magdalene's story is especially significant for her witness to Jesus's resurrection, an event at the heart of Christian faith. (John 20: 1; 11-18)

Mary Magdalene's involvement goes beyond mere observation. According to the Gospel accounts, she was one of the first to discover the empty tomb and, in several accounts, the first to see the risen Jesus. This encounter positions her as a primary witness to the resurrection, tasked with delivering the astonishing news to the other disciples. Her role in these moments challenges and transcends the societal norms of her time, which often limited women's roles in religious and public life.

It is clear from these scriptures that God never had a problem with women in authority. God also obviously calls, appoints, and assigns women to lead. Just from these four women, we can see the power and authority that God placed in their hands.

Whenever a scripture contradicts another, there is no reason to doubt God's word. More often, the meaning of one or the other is lost in translation. On the contrary, we must dig deeper for the correct interpretation. A deeper study of certain words, cultural norms, time periods, and even the author's mission will shed light on the scriptures' original meaning.

Apostle Paul Approves Women In Ministry

Paul was Kingdom-focused; his goal was to preach Christ and unify the body of believers under a common faith. He was also a Jew; therefore, he understood cultural norms. As he delivered God's word, he would need to address those cultural practices to bring unity amongst the Jewish culture. This would mean balancing and correcting wrong behavior practices and adherence to cultural beliefs.

Paul implied in 1 Cor. 11:3-16 that women are permitted to pray and prophesy in church. Keep in mind that the prophetic ministry is of great authority and carries the weight and the responsibility of speaking God's Word to His people of all genders. Therefore, Paul could not have set a universal rule for all women. Because in many other scriptures, he had instructed them on how to present themselves when praying, teaching, or prophesying in church.

Let's shift our attention from the notion of silence to the concept of learning. In the customs of ancient Jewish society, formal education was predominantly reserved for men, who were afforded the privilege of studying religious texts. In contrast, women's roles were generally centered around domestic responsibilities, without the provision for formal education. *(19 December 1999 Karen Rachel, halvi/Hyman Encyclopedia of Jewish Women)*

So why would the apostle Paul have instructed women on how to posture themselves when learning? Why did he say that women should learn in silence? For this reason, we must ask whether he was prohibiting women from speaking or establishing standard guidelines for them to partake in learning.

Apostle Paul introduced something far more significant in the text than silencing women. Instead, he challenged cultural practices that did not emulate God's Kingdom. His message implied that women should be allowed to learn and thus gave them instructions on how to do so. While still honoring Jewish culture.

In this context, the term "silence" isn't used to describe or modify anything, which means it's not functioning as an adjective. Instead, the emphasis is on the concept of learning, to better understand what Paul was addressing with this group of believers. It seems he was tackling a specific issue related to women. However, his guidance appears to be intended for a specific situation, not as a universal directive.

We can validate that by the many instances where Apostle Paul referenced leading women in his letters—even commending them and urging others to help and honor them. Therefore, proving that he was not given a universal command to women everywhere. Below are a few instances where the Apostle Paul honors women:

Phoebe, a Deacon in the church: Paul asked the church to receive her and honor her as an asset to him and the church. "I commend to you our sister Phoebe, a deacon of the church in Cenchreae.

> *"I ask you to receive her in the Lord in a way worthy of his people and to give her any help she may need from you, for she has been the benefactor of many people, including me." – Romans 16:1-2*

Pricilla, The Wife of Aquila: they were a husband-and-wife ministry team. Paul admonished them for their work and commitment to the ministry.

> *"Greet Priscilla and Aquila, my co-workers in Christ Jesus. They risked their lives for me. Not only I but all the churches of the Gentiles are grateful to them. Greet also the church that meets at their house." – Romans 16:3-5*

Nympha: She was the leader of a house church in Lycus Valley. Paul sent her a greeting to acknowledge her work for the Kingdom of God.

> *"Give my greetings to the brothers and sisters at Laodicea, and to Nympha and the church in her house." – Colossians 4:15*

Apphia leader of a house church: The Apostle Paul addressed her in one of the letters as a leader alongside Archippus Philemon.

> *"Paul, a prisoner of Christ Jesus, and Timothy our brother, To Philemon our dear friend and fellow worker—also to Apphia our sister and*

Archippus our fellow soldier—and to the church that meets in your home." – Philemon 1-2

Euodia and Syntyche Paul's Ministry Colleagues: Paul sent word to these two women to peacefully settle their dispute. He commends them as fellow workers (Co-Laborers) alongside him in the Gospel.

"I beseech Euodias, and beseech Syntyche, that they be of the same mind in the Lord. And I entreat thee also, true yokefellow, help those women which laboured with me in the gospel, with Clement also, and with other my fellow-laborers, whose names are in the book of life." - Philippians 4:2-3

Lydia A Worshiper/Converted By Paul's Ministry: Lydia was known for her worship. She was converted by the Apostle Paul's ministry when God altered his original plans to go to Philippi. After she heard the Gospel, she received and asked The Apostle to continue the meetings in her house.

"And a certain woman named Lydia, a seller of purple, of the city of Thyatira, which worshipped God, heard us: whose heart the Lord opened, that she attended unto the things which were spoken of Paul. And when she was baptized, and her household, she besought us, saying, If ye have judged me to be faithful to the Lord, come into my house, and abide there. And she constrained us." – Acts 16:11-15

It is clear from these scriptures that the Apostle Paul did not have a problem with women in ministry or leading in any capacity. If this is true, we must debunk the idea that his instruction to the Corinthian church was a universal order. We must also accept that Paul was dealing with an isolated event.

Isn't it ironic how a few scriptures are used to exclude women and diminish our vital role in advancing God's Kingdom? It is easier to adopt negative connotations of those scriptures when the concept of exclusion is so heavily embedded in our culture. It is even beneficial to some to focus more on the word silence than to accept women's liberation and God-given right to serve alongside men in an equal capacity.

Many cultural traditions concerning women are erroneous due to misinterpretation of God's word. Interpretation can be clouded by the wickedness of man's hearts, conformity to our cultural norms, and blatant disobedience to God. But remember, God is Love. *Therefore, we cannot believe that love would create women (us) merely for diabolical mistreatment and abuse.*

We have not seen the full power and authority women embody nor the magnitude of what we can contribute to advancing God's Kingdom. *For a reason we have yet to embark upon, someone decided that being a girl did not make for a good king.* Cultural beliefs have masked the truth of our inclusion. And the doctrine of men has taught us to be silent even when we are speaking. The burden of the veil of exclusion often places today's women in one of three categories:

SILENT: Remaining subordinate to ridiculous ideas and costumes, highlighting the point that women are the weaker vessels and only called to serve men. I find this to be the cruelest posture a woman can take. In this place, purpose and visions are not explored. Gifts and talents are only necessary to help or benefit a male. Unfortunately, this place leaves little room to follow your passion for the purpose and call of God. But it brings us to an important question—*what will we say to God when He asks us what we did with the talents He gave us?*

"I cry out to God Most High, to God who fulfills his purpose for me." — Psalm 57:2

ANGRY: They become angry once they understand their identity. They preach and teach with a fervor tinged with anger, determined to destroy anything or anyone that has ever stood against equality for them. Yet, it is nothing more than a vile trick of the enemy. Initially, this path seems like the most liberating course of action. Yet, it is nothing more than a vile trick of the enemy.

This anger acts as a shield, designed to prevent them from appearing weak, a form of camouflage intended to mask the pain accompanying their rise from the deep shadows of exclusion. But make no mistake, it is unhealthy, and many sins will arise from the deep root of anger. We must recognize this for what it is: a malicious attempt by our adversary to mock the power and presence of God. The temptation to "get them all told" might feel satisfying at the moment, but we are called to a higher purpose.

We must learn to manage the fire and the power within us, always remembering the love and forgiveness of God. We must remain anchored in His principles. The fire will come, and the power we wield is a gift of God-given grace. However, our willingness to manage it with love demands a disciplined restraint of our flesh.

"Refrain from anger and turn from wrath; do not fret—it leads only to evil." - Psalms 37:8 (NIV)

DISCONNECTED: She Disconnects from any form of fellowship. This disconnection often happens when a woman becomes fed up and mostly tired of fighting what seems to be a never-ending battle. Because she has experienced truth, there will be no turning back to the old—thus, she settles for disconnecting from the organizational church, refusing even to advance the Kingdom of God through her gifts. *She can quickly become bitter, judgmental, and disobedient to God in this place.*

Yet, God has ordained fellowship in some capacity. While a temporary withdrawal may sometimes be necessary for personal growth or healing, it's important to understand the process of disconnecting, detoxifying, and then re-emerging, ready to re-engage with a community of believers. The way you fellowship might change dramatically once the veil of exclusion is lifted. Therefore, we must be open to new expressions of fellowship, whether that means reimagining our approach to Sunday worship or exploring alternative gatherings such as smaller groups, homes, hubs, or networks. Ultimately, the direction for these new paths of fellowship will become clear as we fully embrace our God-given identity and begin to embrace our authority.

> *"And let us consider how to spur one another on to love and good deeds. Let us not neglect meeting together, as some have made a habit, but let us encourage one another, and all the more as you see the Day approaching." —Hebrews 10:25 (BSB)*

First Does Not Mean Better

Unfortunately, women often teach, preach, and lead beneath this veil of exclusion. The idea that we are inferior to men is embedded in our minds. This kind of thinking makes us feel unworthy of our kingship. It is a deep imprint left in the hearts of women that often handicaps our functionality and limits our ability to flow in the graces that God has given us.

The Apostle Paul gave a command for women to be silent. Was this statement all-inclusive? —NO. And did it imply that women could not have leadership roles in the church or pioneer in kingdom developments? —Absolutely not!

Consider this; just because something comes first doesn't make it better. Coming first doesn't mean that what comes after is less or will depreciate. John the Baptist announced the coming of Christ and stated that there was One coming after him that was, in fact, greater than him. (Mark 1:7)

"And he preached, saying, 'There comes One after me who is mightier than I, whose sandal strap I am not worthy to stoop down and loose.'" —Mark 1:7

Moreover, we find our answer to the challenge of the enslavement of women within the pages of God's Holy Scripture. We are fearfully and wonderfully made, crafted by the hands of the Almighty; we inhaled the same breath of God that our male counterparts inhaled. (Psalms 139:14) We are created in the image of our Sovereign God, and God gave woman the same dominion and authority to rule over the earth as He did man.

Scripture proves that God did not create women subservient to men. However, it appears that all creation has embraced its redemption except the woman. Therefore, He sends this revelation of inclusion—yes you are a lady, but you are a king too! And real kings rule with dominion, power, and authority.

Dismantling the Myth About Adam

Let's dismantle some myths about Adam—God's first man. For years, we have heard the stories of Genesis, and for most of us, it was like a fairytale imposed upon us for entertainment by some fictional author. We breezed through it, not thinking about the rich truth of our identity that it carries.

We err in our interpretations of the scripture because we have not learned and understood this first man called Adam. He is often viewed as a piece of creation's puzzle having no rhythm or rhyme as if he merely existed.

Contrary to popular belief, God created Adam as an extraordinary being. He was made in the image of God, endowed with the authority to govern the earth. Moreover, there's an intriguing aspect to his creation—he was one man, yet he represented the entirety of humanity. Within him, Eve (woman) already existed—representing the complete work of the Father and providing proof of His declaration, *'Let us make man in our image, and let them have dominion over the earth."* (Genesis 1:27). It is proof that He is the final word and what He speaks happens.

Adam was all-sufficient. His relationship with God was impeccable. He communed with him daily and thus spoke God's heart into the earthly realm, and God agreed with him. For instance, although God had predestined Eve from the outset, it was Adam who, in Genesis 2:20, articulated the need for her presence.

> *"The Lord God said, "It is not good for the man to be alone. I will make a helper suitable for him."–Genesis 2:18 (KJV)*

For many years, I thought Adam got lonely, and God created Eve to satisfy that loneliness. What a shallow interpretation of such a profound scripture. Looking closely at the beginning of this scripture, God decided that it was not good for man to be alone (Verse 18). God, the omniscient (all-knowing) One, decides that man needs something more.

It is my solemn belief that God makes no mistakes and that He does everything for a reason. Suppose the earth was carefully thought out and orchestrated by Him to suit the man He had in mind. Then one must consider that if He was adding something, it had to be life-sustaining for humanity. We must also understand that it was far greater than the male's need for someone to cook for him, have sex with him, clean for him, bow to him, submit to him, or bear children for him. God's plan for His daughters is much deeper than this shallow perception that the world sometimes has of us.

God stopped the progression of humanity on the earth to introduce the woman. He decided it would be wrong if she did not enter the scene. And without her, there would be no helper for humanity—wow!

It is in God's nature to love humanity and care for us—His love is unconditional. Thus, He plans for our future and establishes help when He knows that danger lies ahead. Imagine if you could foresee your children's future. Would you not attempt to prevent all the bad things? And if prevention were impossible, wouldn't you at least strive to create a path for their recovery? In many ways, this is what God did for humanity when He created woman—He sent help!

Introducing the Helpmeet

As I have mentioned, God does not err; if something is added or introduced, it is by God's design. If there was a need to create or introduce something later, it was due to human deficiency, not a shortfall on God's part.

In Part B of Genesis 2:18, God declares, *"I will make him an help meet for him."* This phrase, *'help meet,'* often combined into *'helpmeet,'* has obscured a critical aspect of women's rich inheritance in the Kingdom of

God. Furthermore, the misinterpretation of this term has contributed to the significant degradation of women. Therefore, we must take a more in-depth look at the term "help meet." We must restore its original meaning and eliminate this unjust excuse for the exclusion of women from God's plans.

Help-Meet =Ezer-Ke-negdo Strong's #5828 (**Hebrew = ezer**) aid: -- help Strong's Root = # 5826 (Hebrew = azar) prime root: to surround, i.e., protect or aid: help, (**Hebrew = kenegdo**) corresponding to, counterpart to, equal to matching.

First, let's adopt a practical viewpoint. If dominion alone could satisfy Adam, wouldn't the animals have sufficed? He had authority over them, and they obeyed him. The interaction between Eve and the serpent suggests some form of communication was possible between humans and animals.

Yet, there was still something missing for Adam. God had predestined Eve's arrival even before Adam realized he required more than just the animals' companionship (Genesis 2:18). Thus, Adam's need for Eve was not a deviation but a fulfillment of God's original plan.

The Hebrew definition of the word helpmeet is Ezer Kenegdo: The meaning of the Hebrew word Ezer is a helper. And Kenegdo is a counterpart, corresponding to, equal to, or a match.

God had given Adam someone equal to him in authority and dominion. Therefore, she was able to satisfy him. Assuming that Adam refers to Eve's suitableness for him because she was taken out of him will misinterpret this scripture. It was much deeper than that. Eve was suitable for Adam because she was in the original plan of God for him.

Accepting the Hebrew word *Ezer Kenegdo in* its English form alone does not do it justice. Instead, it takes on a slightly negative connotation and presents the image of someone less than or secondary to the other. However, the opposite is true; Eve was far from being merely secondary to Adam. She was his equal, his mirror in essence and purpose. Adam's initial reaction upon seeing Eve—declaring her 'flesh of my flesh and bone of my bone'—reflects a recognition of their profound unity and equality.

When looking back at Genesis 2:18, when Adam named the animals, the scripture states that Adam did not find anyone suitable for him. Adam was implying that there was no other earthly creature like him. He was not longing for a servant or someone to play housewife to him. Adam desired someone just like him. His need to rule over something had already been fulfilled, as he had complete authority over every living creature. Eve was his equal; she was the one whom he could communicate with, have dominion and authority with—she could subdue alongside him.

They were both created in the image of God. Just as God looked at the man endowed with His attributes and saw His reflection, thus deemed His work good. When Adam the man looked at Eve, he saw his reflection. (which was God's reflection) Eve was a direct replica of Adam; except she was the female version. Therefore, Adam declared Eve was bone of his bone and flesh of his flesh—it was like looking in a mirror. How could Eve ever be beneath Adam if she indeed bore the same image of God as him?

To imply that the woman is weaker than the man would be like saying that God is weak, as the man is the direct image of God, and the woman is the direct image of man. Therefore, they are both made in God's image.

Thus, the Ezer-Kenegdo came on the scene for a reason. It wasn't just to serve her male counterpart. She bore the image of God as a strong, militant helper. The female's function differs from the male's function, but not her power or authority. She is different from the man because she possesses the womb—she can give birth. She is feminine to the touch, graceful, and poised but she is by no means less than him.

She had to enter the scene because Satan was already in the Garden (Ezekiel 28:13). God being all-knowing, saw this in advance and said it is not good for man to be all-one; I will make him a helper—someone to rescue him. The woman is not just a helper for her husband. She was brought forth as a helper for humanity. She is the vehicle Christ used to enter the earth—through her womb redemption was born.

Satan knew the woman's purpose. He also knew that she was a threat to him. I believe that this is the reason that he pursued her. For this reason, we can never look at ourselves as inferior again. We are rulers endowed with power and a militant zeal to destroy the very kingdom of Satan.

Because our very existence is a threat to Satan's kingdom, he keeps coming after us with everything he has. But it is for this exact reason that Ezer-Kenegdo is about to overthrow his reign again. In this hour, women are called to massively advance the kingdom of God. However, to do so we must own our identity as Lady Kings on the earth. We must purpose to uproot, dig out, launch, lay a foundation, set order, and overthrow Satan's debauchery, which now has the ecclesia spinning in a circle.

It is as if we are watching a clown show in most of our services today. The adversary is having a field-day with what I call new-age religion. However, the remnant is arising—it just so happens that once again God's daughter will bring the report (even as Mary Magdelene did)—He isn't dead! He is alive! Come see!

Lady King Verses Lady Queen

And hath made us kings and priests unto God and his Father; to him be glory and dominion forever and ever. Amen. - Revelation 1:6 (KJV)

The term 'lady king' carries an oddity within itself. Whenever I mention it, it invariably elicits a look of confusion. This confusion stems mainly from our traditional understanding of a king. A basic internet search on the definition of a king will reveal that a king is a male monarch. The emphasis on 'male' often precedes any discussion of the role's functions or characteristics that true kingship embodies.

The definition creates a mental picture of a male in authority. Therefore, when we hear the word king, we subconsciously envision a male in authority. Thus, many have challenged me by asking why not call ourselves queens. They argue that "a queen is simply a female version of a king." That sounds good; however, it is untrue.

The Hebrew word queen is Shegal which means the king's wife, or Gebhirah, queen mother (It is a term of endearment bestowed upon a royal lady—someone acquainted with the king (i.e. the king's mother). For example, the king's mother may be called queen-mother because of her relationship with the king. The term doesn't mean the same as a monarch (malakah)—one ruling like a king, such as [7]Queen Sheba.

Therefore, as a queen, she may influence the king in some way. However, she does not have absolute authority. She is limited in her rule-ship

[7] Queen Sheba embodied the qualities and responsibilities of a monarch similar to that of a king, despite the gender-specific titles of the period. Her legacy as a powerful and wise ruler transcends the distinction between king and queen, highlighting her significant role in the ancient world. (1 Kings 10:1-13; 2 Chronicles 9:1-12),

because she is still subordinate to the king. For example, the biblical story of Queen Esther is a beautiful way to differentiate between a queen and a king. (Esther chapter 3-7)

Although Esther was the queen and very influential with the king, she in no way possessed the king's authority. She could only use her influence over him to make her petition to the king in hopes of persuading him to fulfill her wishes.

Had Esther's authority as queen been equal to that of the kings, she would have had the same power as the king with or without his approval. However, she had no power to decree a matter, with the assurance that it would be obeyed without the king's approval. Therefore, with all her influence, our beloved Esther was still the king's wife with limited authority. (Esther Chpt. 7) Now, this in no way diminishes her. In any case, we can argue that everyone was subject to the king's final approval. Nonetheless, this example seems fitting to demonstrate the difference between the two.

Our identity can only be proven and understood by our relationship with God—our eternal King. He is the creator, and the creator knows the purpose of what He created. He is our Father, and we are His sons. (John 1:12) As odd as this may seem, we are neither male nor female in the spirit (Galatians 3:28).

If this is so, He has made us kings and priests (Rev. 1:6). Most of us cannot accept that we are kings because we fail to look past the gender specifics of the world's definition of a king. In the realm of the spirit, and according to God's eternal law being a king has absolutely nothing to do with being male or female. On the other hand, it has everything to do with dominion, power, and authority.

The Definition of A King

The following definitions of a king are pulled from three reputable dictionary sources. Upon their first examination, we see that the primary definition is that a king should be a male.

• **The male ruler of an independent state,** especially one who inherits the position by right of birth. (Oxford dictionaries.com)

• **A male monarch of a major territorial unit;** especially one whose position is hereditary and who rules for life (Merriam Webster)

• **A male ruler of a nation or state usually called a kingdom;** male sovereign, limited or absolute; monarch (Dictonary.com)

All pulled from different sources, they each describe a king as a male first before indicating the king's domain, dominion, power, or authority. However, removing the word male from the above definitions will provide a more definitive understanding of a king's identity, apart from his gender. Several things stand out:

The king is a ruler of a domain: When God created mankind, meaning both male and female, He gave the earth as their place to rule or their domain (Genesis 1:28). Mankind was given dominion over every living thing but not over each other—God speaks to the heavenly host man's identity (uniqueness, individuality, distinctiveness, personality). He did not add a gender clause. Therefore, our identity is our uniqueness in the earthly realm. It is the delegated authority that God has given both males and females to be the absolute supreme authority in the earth. No other living creature can embody this type of power on the earth.

The king's authority is given to him by birthright: Kingship is inherited. The son is the inheritor of the kingdom—not a son by gender but a son by the spirit.

> *There is neither Jew nor Greek; there is neither bond nor free, there is neither male nor female: for ye are all one in Christ Jesus. -Galatians 3:28 (KJV)*

> *Beloved, now are we the sons of God, and it doth not yet appear what we shall be: but we know that, when He shall appear, we shall be like him; for we shall see him as he is. -1 John 3:2 (KJV)*

The king rules for life: The kingdom belongs to the king for life and will not be taken away. God has given mankind the earth as his domain.

> *The heaven, even the heavens, are the Lord's: but the earth hath he given to the children of men. -Psalm 115:16 (KJV)*

He is sovereign: The king is the dominant one in the kingdom. He is superior to all that is under him. And his power is unmatched except by another king.

> *What is mankind that you are mindful of them, human beings that you care for them? You have made them a little lower than the angels and crowned them with glory and honor. You made them rulers over the works of your hands; you put everything under their feet: - Psalm 8:4-6 (NIV).*

The true *Lady King* transcends gender; she is defined by sonship. Ironically this sonship has nothing to do with cultural beliefs or societal norms—and even less to do with gender. No man can give us the right to be sons—God has already spoken—we are His sons, and His word is final.

If God had intended for Eve to be subservient to Adam, He would have explicitly stated so in His original plan. Instead, as scripture clearly articulates, God's intentions for humanity were to establish two rulers of equal power and strength. This revelation does not diminish the male's role; rather, it proclaims an ancient truth, symbolizing the return of a crown to a king. It is a call for the crowning of women as 'lady kings,' symbolizing our rightful ascension to positions of honor, power, and authority alongside our male counterparts, in equal rulership as originally intended by God.

Consider these two profound questions: How can you lose something you never possessed in the first place? And if it were the female's destiny to be subservient to the male, how could it possibly be her punishment? Isn't a punishment typically something that takes one out of their comfort zone, something uncomfortable or hard to manage?

Dear Lady Kings, remember this: Your gender is female, but your God-given identity on this Earth is dominion, power, and authority—kingship. You stand superior to those things created for you. You hold dominion and power. You are Ezer Kenegdo to your Man-King—you are a power equal to him.

May you embrace the redemption of Christ, your God-given authority to make your own choices, and the wisdom to choose life" –Selah.

Highlights of A Lady King

02: The Revelation of Inclusion | Sojourner Truth (1797-)

Abolitionist and Advocate for Women's Rights

"And ain't I a woman? Look at me! Look at my arm! I have ploughed and planted, and gathered into barns, and no man could head me! And ain't I a woman?

—Sojourner Truth

Sojourner Truth, born Isabella Baumfree, was a remarkable African American woman who lived during the 19th century in the United States. Her life story and powerful speeches continue to inspire people around the world, emphasizing the significance of reclaiming one's voice in the fight for justice and equality.

Born into slavery in 1797 in Swartekill, New York, Sojourner Truth's early years were marked by unimaginable hardships and suffering. She was separated from her family at a young age and subjected to the brutalities of slavery. However, in 1826, she managed to escape to freedom with her infant daughter, embarking on a journey that would shape her destiny.

After gaining her freedom, Isabella Baumfree became Sojourner Truth and devoted her life to advocating for the abolition of slavery and women's rights. She emerged as a powerful and passionate speaker, addressing audiences across the United States. One of her most famous speeches, "Ain't I a Woman?" delivered in 1851 at the Women's Rights Convention in Akron, Ohio, challenged prevailing notions of gender and racial equality. In her speech, she eloquently argued for the rights of both African

American women and all women, underscoring their strength and resilience.

Sojourner Truth's dedication to justice and equality made her a prominent figure in the abolitionist and women's suffrage movements. Her authenticity and powerful oratory skills earned her respect and admiration from her contemporaries and continue to inspire generations of activists today.

Throughout her life, Sojourner Truth demonstrated the profound impact that a single voice can have in the struggle for human rights. Her legacy serves as a reminder of the importance of using one's voice to challenge injustice and fight for a more equitable society.

02: Chapter | Expounding More on the Ezer Kenegdo

Ezer Kenegdo is a Hebrew term found in the Bible, specifically in the book of Genesis (Genesis 2:18). It is often translated as "helper suitable" or "help meet" in traditional English translations. However, this translation doesn't fully capture the depth and significance of the original Hebrew term.

Ezer: This word means "helper" or "help." It signifies support, aid, and assistance. Importantly, the term "ezer" is not a subservient or inferior role but conveys the idea of a strong and necessary help.

Kenegdo: This word is often translated as "suitable for" or "fit for." It implies complementarity or a corresponding partner. It indicates that the helper is not inferior but aligns with and complements the other.

Together, Ezer Kenegdo suggests a profound partnership where the woman is a strong and essential helper who stands alongside the man as an equal partner, complementing and corresponding to him in God's creation. This concept challenges traditional interpretations that might have diminished the role of women.

Ezer Kenegdo emphasizes the shared responsibility and shared dominion given to both men and women in their divine purpose and calling.

The journey to recovery is not without its challenges. The scars of history run deep, and the adversary remains relentless. Yet, armed with the promise of redemption and the knowledge of our unique role as God's daughters, we are in pursuit of total restoration.

Photo Credit: Rich Allela and Dapel Kureng

Chapter 03

The Magnitude of the Loss

Unto the woman he said, I will greatly multiply thy sorrow and thy conception; in sorrow, thou shalt bring forth children; thy desire shall be to thy husband, and he shall rule over thee. —Genesis 3:16 (KJV)

From one decade to the next, we have struggled to reclaim what we lost in the Garden of Eden. However, to truly understand this loss, we must retrace our identity in Christ as it was before the fall. Our ability to function in authority as 'lady kings' on earth today hinges on fully grasping the magnitude of power, dominion, and authority we were originally granted. This deep understanding is crucial for us to adequately walk in our identity and embody the fullness of what it means to be God's daughters.

It is not only crucial to understand what we lost, but also to uncover the mastermind behind that attack. We must unravel both the purpose and the plan of this assault, recognizing the profound reason why the enemy targeted the 'lady king's' position. Acknowledging the severity of satan's attack on women is imperative, as failing to do so leads to an underestimation of the fall's impact—not just for women but for humanity as a whole.

God created mankind, both male and female, to work together, rule together, and exercise dominion over the earth together (Genesis 1:27-28). Even when separated, they were expected to collaborate. There was no hierarchy between them; both were sovereign and held equal authority on the earth.

Their partnership fulfilled a divine mandate. They were created as one in the flesh but separated for redemption's purpose and companionship. They were commanded to rule the earth, having complete dominion and authority (Genesis 2:18, 24). While capable of functioning individually, together they embodied dunamis power[8] on the earth. This represented the complete work of God's beloved humanity, which equipped both males and females to act as ruling authorities on the earth (Ecclesiastes 4:9-12).

When sin entered the hearts of Adam and Eve, it shook our earthly kingdom (Genesis 3:6-7), altering the woman's position and authority in a manner that remains only partially rectified even today. For example, despite the price of our redemption being paid, we often find ourselves living in a state of bondage. We portray a semblance of freedom, yet we are still constrained by the consequences of Eve's decision. We are partially restored and at times acknowledged, but not fully free to embrace our God-given identity and authority in the Earth.

Building upon the foundation of Christ's sacrifice for our complete freedom (Galatians 5:1), it is essential to recognize that, at times, this liberty appears suppressed, seemingly awaiting our full realization and embrace of our roles as God's daughters and as true 'lady kings.' As we journey

[8] Dunamis power, derived from the Greek word "δύναμις" (dunamis), refers to strength, power, or ability. In a biblical context, it is often associated with the power of God manifested in miracles, healing, and other supernatural acts. Dunamis is not just any power; it's a divine power that goes beyond human capabilities, enabling believers to perform works that reflect God's power and authority.

towards the full knowledge of this profound truth, all of creation eagerly anticipates our awakening (Romans 8:19). This anticipation speaks to a pivotal moment where the advancement of the Kingdom of God and greater gatherings of true believers hinge upon us—women, daughters, sons, and kings—embracing our God-given identity and delivering a decisive, power-filled blow to the kingdom of darkness.

The tragedy of our collective loss as women in the fall has obscured our vision, hindering our progress and dimming the recognition of our fundamental worth as daughters and heirs of the Kingdom. Thus, we are called—beckoned, even summoned—to action, urging us to delve deeper into the magnitude of what we lost, to reclaim it, and to step into our rightful place of authority once more.

Function vs. Superiority

To fully grasp what was lost due to sin, it is crucial to differentiate between functions and superiority, in the same way, we distinguish between being first and being greater. This concept is illustrated in the biblical story of John the Baptist, the forerunner of Christ. When announcing Christ's coming, John stated, 'There is one coming after me who is greater than I' (John 1:27). This statement highlights the distinction between order and greatness; Christ, coming after John, was deemed greater, not because of the sequence but due to His divine nature and mission.

Similarly, when looking at the story of creation, we shouldn't assume that being created first makes someone automatically superior. Although Adam was created first, this does not imply that God's original plan was for Adam to rule over Eve. Genesis 1:27 shows that both were created in God's image and given dominion and power on the earth. Thus, this story presents them as partners, with distinct but complementary roles, without implying a hierarchy of value or authority.

Therefore, it's essential to understand that the sequential order in creation does not equate to a divine endorsement of superiority. Just as John the Baptist's role was to prepare the way for one greater than himself, the creation sequence in Genesis also had a divine purpose. However, it in no way implies or establishes a hierarchy of worth or dominion and authority between Adam and Eve.

When Eve was created from Adam, there was a shift in their roles. Adam was no longer the sole supreme being with the ability to perform all functions. Eve represented the female aspect of Adam and, as such, possessed the womb, making her capable of giving birth. This was one of her functions, not because she was inferior to Adam, but because it was her unique role.

Every pre-fall account regarding humanity suggests that Eve was anything but inferior or insignificant. Logically, if one seeks to conquer, overthrow, bring down, or eradicate something, weakening its most powerful element is essential. For example, aiming to destroy a tree involves more than just cutting it down; merely doing so might not ensure its permanent removal. Uprooting it, however, eliminates its ability to reproduce, ensuring it never returns. Thus, if the enemy intended to control the kingdom of earth and ensure that his actions in the garden would persist across generations, he had to attack or attach himself to the most powerful part of humanity.

Take a Deeper Look!

Ladies, I implore you to closely examine the dynamics surrounding the Fall. While God had commanded both Adam and Eve not to eat from the tree of the knowledge of good and evil, Genesis 3 reveals the role that the serpent played in this event. It also outlines his characteristics, stating that he was the most cunning and crafty of all creatures. These very attributes align with those of Satan. Scripture even suggests that he can masquerade as an angel of light (2 Corinthians 11:14).

His warfare against humanity is strategic and meticulously planned. He exercises patience, which is a valuable trait in times of battle, choosing his moments to force individuals to deviate from God's plan and purpose for their lives. He never settles for partial victories; every element of his attack is a precisely planned assault.

Why Beguile Eve and Not Adam

Recognizing Satan's strategic nature in his attacks leads us to believe that his assault on Eve was more than a mere opportunity. He had a greater objective. His primary intent was not just to entice Eve into disobedience; he planned to overthrow an entire kingdom and its government—He wanted Earth. However, according to divine law, the only way, he could rule it was through the heart of man.

But what made Eve so precious that the serpent beguiled her instead of Adam? Did he choose Eve because she was weaker? Or did it all happen by chance — was Eve in the right place but at the wrong time? These questions have weighed heavily on my mind for some time, and I believe they warrant an answer.

Beguile: Such a definition suggests that Satan's persuasion of Eve went far beyond a simple suggestion. This beguiling was not a mere request; it was the work of a skilled opponent who had pursued the woman relentlessly. After the events had unfolded, Eve was left to face the consequences of submitting to Satan.

Consider the statement I made earlier in this chapter about distinct functions. Remember, Eve is Adam with a womb. One of her functions, let me emphasize, one of her functions, was to give birth. Satan's primary ambition was to be like God, leading to his eviction from heaven along with a third of the angels. Consider Isaiah 14:12-14:

"How art thou fallen from heaven, O Lucifer, son of the morning! how art thou cut down to the ground, which didst weaken the nations! For thou hast said in thine heart, I will ascend into heaven, I will exalt my throne above the stars of God: I will sit also upon the mount of the congregation, in the sides of the north: I will ascend above the heights of the clouds; I will be like the most High" (Isaiah 14:12-14, KJV).

Satan desired to rule the earthly kingdom, and Eve played a pivotal role in achieving this goal. Contrary to popular belief, he did not target Eve because she was the weaker link but because of her unique function. She possessed the ability to accomplish for him what Adam could not—giving birth to a wicked nation of people. And so, he beguiled her.

The word "beguiles" means to charm or enchant someone, sometimes in a deceptive way, or to trick someone into doing something (dictionary.com). Such a definition suggests that Satan's persuasion of Eve went far beyond a simple suggestion. This beguiling was not a mere request; it was the work of a skilled opponent who had pursued the woman relentlessly. After the events had unfolded, Eve was left to face the consequences of submitting to Satan.

Genesis 3:16 describes Eve's punishment: "In pain, you shall bring forth children, and your desire shall be for your husband, and he shall rule over you." While there is much debate on the interpretation of this scripture, one underlying truth remains—something changed for God's woman that day.

Eve's position had been significantly altered. Everything she was created to be had been torn from her. Originally, she was created equal to Adam, ruling with him, having dominion, and conquering alongside him. However, the misuse of her earthly authority had consequences that persisted through every generation. Thus, long after the finished work of the cross, women still bear the wounds of that fall. The question that echoes through the corridors of history is this: Can our crown ever be recovered? If so, will it ever be recovered?

Why Satan Hates Women

It would seem that a shattered image or identity is punishment enough. The penalty appeared too great for one gender to bear. God's woman, the Ezer Kenegdo had been far removed from her position of power and Authority. She went from a conqueror to the conquered, from an equal to a subordinate. Yet, there was more to come. This one act of disobedience placed the woman in constant combat with Satan himself. *Genesis 3:15 (KJV) states, 'And I will put enmity between thee and the woman, and between thy seed and her seed; it shall bruise thy head, and thou shalt bruise his heel.'*

The term 'enmity' should not be taken lightly. Further exploration of Genesis 3:15 seems to confirm that this command from God was both a punishment and a promise of redemption. It marked the beginning of a war between what once seemed like two allies.

It may be unsettling to think of Eve as once an ally to Satan, but let's consider the definition of an ally: *a partner, an assistant, or a helper.* In her interaction with Satan, Eve embodied these roles, aiding him in achieving his objectives. He established a relationship with her and presented an argument that enticed her. Consequently, Eve partnered with him in defying God's command.

Amid this conflict, a promise emerged, as captured in the profound words of Genesis 3:15: *'And I will put enmity between you and the woman, and between your offspring and hers; he will crush your head, and you will strike his heel' (KJV).*

This scripture speaks of a relentless enmity and unyielding hostility between the woman and the head of the serpent (Satan). Let's examine these words carefully. The enmity, as described, would be between Eve and the head of the serpent, as well as between their respective offspring. This extends far beyond the moment in the Garden of Eden. Not only would Satan harbor hatred towards the woman, but all who embraced the ways of Satan—his offspring—would also despise the offspring of the woman.

While we could delve deeper into this topic, for the sake of this text, I will focus on a fundamental understanding. In this context, the woman's offspring refers to Jesus. She was destined to give birth to humanity's redemption. Therefore, as Jesus represents redemption from the Fall for all humanity, all who favor the works of Satan would inherently oppose

Jesus Christ.The question, "Can our crown ever be recovered?" is met with a resounding affirmation—an affirmation that echoes through the ages. Yes, the crown can be recovered, and indeed, it will be.

Our journey toward reclaiming the crown transcends the mere regaining of lost ground; it heralds a new era where women, fully restored and empowered, will comprehend the full depth of our authority and the divine right we possess to walk in purpose.

The War on Women is Different

The war on women is unlike any other conflict ever waged. Disguised beneath the darkness of the woman's fall, Satan has enlisted agents to work on his behalf in concealing our true identity. He wields power over wickedness in high places, employing cunning tactics to influence lawmakers and legislation to align with his plan to suppress the authority of God's daughter.

This war transcends ethnicity, nationality, religion, and political affiliation. It is waged irrespective of skin color. Led by Satan himself, its primary agenda is to keep the Ezer-Kenegdo in a fallen state. He desires her silence and aims to diminish her identity to that of a mere housewife, a sex object, a kitchen aid, or a servant.

Consider, for instance, the way laws have been shaped across the decades and enforced in various societies. Discriminatory legislation and policies have limited women's access to education, economic opportunities, and even basic rights. Such laws, influenced by the subtle hand of the adversary, have perpetuated gender inequality and suppressed the distinctive strength of God's daughters.[9]

Yet, amid this relentless battle, a glimmer of hope emerges. The Ezer Kenegdo, by the divine will of God, will rise from the ashes of her fallen state. She will not only regain her identity as a conqueror and equal partner but also rediscover her role as a bearer of nations and generations.

As women worldwide awaken to their unique destinies, they will become agents of deliverance, ushering in a new era where the world witnesses the power of women birthing not only children but also ministries, movements, businesses, organizations, books, and a future free from the chains of oppression.

This war, with all its cunning and darkness, will ultimately be overcome by the resilient spirit of the Ezer-Kenegdo. The battle is fierce, but victory is assured, as women arise to fulfill their divine purpose and restore the crown of authority and equality that was ordained for us from the beginning.

"Lady Kings, may you always be aware of the devices of the enemy. May you increase in wisdom and strength. So that you may successfully overthrow the kingdom of darkness."—Selah.

---

[9] See Page 80 For Discriminatory Laws Against Women (A Broader View)

A Broader View

Discriminatory Laws Against Women

The list below is a collection of laws that have directly affected equality between males and females. These pieces of legislation are proof that our battle for equality has continued for decades.

1. **Voting Rights**: In the United States, the 19th Amendment granted women the right to vote in 1920. However, this right primarily benefited white women, as women of color often faced barriers in exercising their voting rights. For example, Mississippi did not ratify the 19th Amendment until 1984, long after it became federal law (Artisan Law).
2. **Marriage and Divorce Rights:** In Israel, divorce depends solely on the will of the husband. Similarly, in Mali, a law mandates a wife's obedience to her husband and declares that women must wait three months to get remarried after a divorce or death; men have no such restriction (ONE.org US).
3. **Workplace Discrimination**: In countries like Cameroon and Guinea, men have more say in where their wives work than the women themselves. For instance, in Cameroon, a husband can prohibit his wife from taking a job in a different trade or profession than him if he feels it is in the best interest of his marriage and children (ONE.org US).
4. **Domestic Violence:** There are 46 countries that have no laws protecting women from domestic violence (ONE.org US).
5. **Work Restrictions Based on Gender**: In China, women are

forbidden from working in mines and performing certain types of physical labor. Russia has similar laws that prevent women from engaging in hard, dangerous, or unhealthy trades, affecting 456 types of work in total (ONE.org US).

6. **Citizenship Rights:** In at least 22 countries, married women cannot pass citizenship to their children as fathers can, and 44 countries do not allow married women to pass citizenship to their spouses as married men can. In the United States, there are additional requirements for a child born out of wedlock to a foreign mother and American father to obtain American citizenship (ONE.org US).
7. **Gender Pay Gap:** The Equal Pay Act of 1963 in the U.S. aimed to address wage discrimination based on gender. Despite this, women, especially Black women and other women of color, often faced continued wage disparities due to loopholes and systemic discrimination (Artisan Law).
8. **Pregnancy Discrimination:** The Pregnancy Discrimination Act of 1978 in the U.S. was intended to prohibit discrimination in the workplace based on pregnancy. However, complaints about pregnancy discrimination increased significantly in the following decades, with many requests for pregnancy accommodations being denied (Artisan Law).
9. **Child Marriage:** Globally, there are places where underage girls are forced into marriage. This practice is prevalent in various countries, contributing to gender discrimination and the violation of girls' rights (DW).

Highlights of A Lady King

03: The Magnitude of The Loss | Harriet Tubman Underground Railroad Conductor (1822)

"I freed a thousand slaves. I could have freed a thousand more if only they knew they were slaves."—Harriet Tubman

Harriet Tubman, born around 1822 in Dorchester County, Maryland, was a remarkable African American abolitionist, humanitarian, and Union spy during the American Civil War. Her life story is a testament to courage, resilience, and unwavering commitment to the cause of freedom.

Harriet Tubman was born into slavery, and her early life was marked by the brutal hardships of forced labor. However, she escaped slavery in 1849, embarking on a perilous journey north to freedom. Her escape was not the end of her story but the beginning of a lifelong mission to help others achieve their freedom.

Tubman soon became a "conductor" on the Underground Railroad, a network of safe houses and secret routes that assisted enslaved individuals in escaping to the North. For nearly a decade, she made approximately 19 trips back into the South, risking her life to guide hundreds of enslaved people to freedom. Her deep knowledge of the landscape, her extraordinary courage, and her strong faith in God made her a legendary figure among abolitionists.

During the Civil War, Tubman worked as a nurse, cook, and spy for the Union Army. Her knowledge of the South and her ability to move discreetly through enemy territory made her an invaluable asset. She also played a crucial role in the Combahee River Raid, a military operation that liberated more than 700 enslaved people.

After the war, Harriet Tubman continued her advocacy for civil rights and women's suffrage. She worked alongside prominent suffragists like Susan B. Anthony and Elizabeth Cady Stanton, highlighting the intersection of racial and gender discrimination. Tubman's dedication to these causes never wavered, and she delivered powerful speeches on the importance of equal rights for all.

In recognition of her extraordinary contributions, Tubman became an icon of the abolitionist movement and a symbol of resistance against oppression. She was widely admired for her fearlessness, compassion, and determination to make the world a better place. In 2020, it was announced that Harriet Tubman's likeness would grace the new design of the U.S. $20 bill, making her the first African American woman to be featured on U.S. currency.

The term "Underground Railroad" is believed to have first been used in a Washington newspaper in 1839, quoting a young slave hoping to escape to freedom. The network's origins can be traced to the late 18th century, and it grew steadily until the Emancipation Proclamation was signed by President Abraham Lincoln. By 1850, it is estimated that approximately 100,000 slaves had escaped to freedom via the Underground Railroad.
Harriet Tubman is the most famous conductor associated with the Underground Railroad. Born an enslaved woman named Araminta Ross, she escaped from a plantation in Maryland in 1849, later returning to rescue family members and others, guiding them to safety in Canada.
https://www.history.com/topics/black-history/underground-railroad

Harriet Tubman's legacy endures as an inspiration to those who continue to fight for justice, equality, and human rights. Her life serves as a reminder that one person, armed with unwavering conviction and compassion, can make an indelible mark on history, and change the course of a nation.

Biblical Example

Queen Esther

Book Of Esther Chapter 2

Perhaps you were born for such a time as this," Esther 4:14.

Esther, the main character in the Book of Esther in the Hebrew Bible, is celebrated for her courage and strategic thinking, which played a pivotal role in saving her people, the Jews, from persecution in the Persian Empire.

The story unfolds in the Persian city of Susa, where Esther, a young Jewish woman, is taken to the palace of King Ahasuerus (Xerxes I) after he deposes his previous queen, Vashti. Esther, whose Jewish identity is initially concealed, finds favor in the eyes of the king and is crowned queen.

The crisis in the narrative arises when Haman, an advisor to the king, devises a plot to kill all Jews in the empire due to his hatred for Mordecai, Esther's cousin, and guardian, who had refused to bow to Haman. Mordecai learns of this plan and appeals to Esther to use her influence to save her people. Despite the risk to her own life, since approaching the king without being summoned could result in death, Esther demonstrates remarkable courage and wisdom in her response.

Esther requests all the Jews in Susa to fast for three days before she approaches the king. Then, she invites both the king and Haman to a series of banquets. At the second banquet, she reveals her Jewish identity and exposes Haman's plot to annihilate her people. The king, enraged by Haman's conspiracy, orders Haman's execution.

The king then allows Esther and Mordecai to write a decree giving the Jews the right to defend themselves against their enemies. This leads to the Jews' victory over their adversaries and the establishment of the festival of Purim, a time of joyful celebration commemorating their deliverance.

Esther's story is one of faith, bravery, and political acumen. Her actions demonstrate the potential of individual agency and courage in the face of systemic injustice and resonate as a powerful example of advocacy and resilience. The Book of Esther thus serves as an inspiring narrative that highlights the role of women in biblical history and the importance of standing up for one's people and beliefs.

Esther's ascension to queenship after Queen Vashti is deposed is detailed in *Esther 2:17, "And the king loved Esther above all the women, and she obtained grace and favour in his sight more than all the virgins; so that he set the royal crown upon her head and made her queen instead of Vashti."*

Key Scripture Highlighting Esther's Boldness and Her Challenge to Traditional Norms.

Esther 4:16, "Go, gather together all the Jews that are present in Shushan, and fast ye for me, and neither eat nor drink three days, night or day: I also and my maidens will fast likewise; and so will I go in unto the king, which is not according to the law: and if I perish, I perish.

The existence of the war on women cannot be denied. Our struggles are deeply etched in history—not just black or white history, but world history.

Photo Credit: **Rich Allela** and **Dapel Kureng**

Chapter 04

The Fight to Recover

At that time, I will deal with all who oppressed you. I will rescue the lame; I will gather the exiles. I will give them praise and honor in every land where they have suffered shame. At that time, I will gather you; at that time, I will bring you home. I will give you honor and praise among all the peoples of the earth when I restore your fortunes before your very eyes," says the Lord.

—Zephaniah 3:16-20 (NIV)

This powerful promise from Zephaniah sets the stage for our ongoing battle—the fight for the liberation and recognition of women everywhere. The belief in the inferiority of women to men has been a relentless force, cascading from generation to generation. While we have reclaimed some aspects of our authority, a significant part remains obscured beneath layers of religious, traditional, and political barriers. The emergence of 'Lady Kings' is crucial in bringing these hidden truths to light, for they have been fiercely contested and must be just as fiercely dismantled.

We bear the battle scars as evidence of our long-standing war against our adversary, with many of us still healing from the wounds of injustice inflicted upon us. We have been viciously pursued by the enemy and often overtaken due to our ignorance of these injustices. Societal norms have conditioned us to adjust or conform to a way of life that doesn't reflect our true identity. All too readily, we have slipped into roles like the subservient wife, the overlooked silent partner, or the proficient yet undervalued employee. In many cases, it has become second nature for us to bow our heads in a posture of servitude, welcoming those among us to treat us like slaves rather than daughters and kings.

Still, many know this war on women exists but remain silent. Those are the ones who have become complacent in the fight, believing that it is impossible to conquer. So, they have retreated and given in to the status quo. They are frustrated, and they are tired. Some fought for equality but were met with opposition by their sisters along the way. It is a daunting task. After all, how does one march forward toward victory when the opposing forces are sometimes those for whom you are fighting?

For example, during the 19th Century, women were fighting for the right to vote. Some women stood in opposition to the movement, afraid to move forward, believing that equality between males and females would somehow impair their womanhood. So, they actively opposed their sisters as they mounted the frontlines of the battlefields, determined to fight for what shouldn't have been taken away. Despite this harsh reality, many marched on. Eventually, they secured women the right to vote. Albeit I can only imagine the many who must have given up entirely when met with opposition from another woman.

It is a very intentional and strategically planned war move to pit one soldier of the same battle platoon against the other. It causes confusion and doubt. If launched at the right time, it can set the entire platoon against each other, thus allowing the enemy control of the battle. This powerful war tactic can and will manifest through fear, jealousy, envy, insecurities, and rejection.

In Chapter Five, ' Unmasking the Wounded Lady King,' we will delve into more in-depth details of how, when, and why some women often fight against other women who are fighting for freedom for them as well. This is the opposition that comes to wage war from within.

The War on Women Cannot Be Ignored

No one can justifiably deny the existence of the war on women. Our struggles are deeply embedded in history—not just in Black or White history but in world history. Regardless of the country you visit, a brief search or inquiry will soon reveal the profound scars left by the injustices endured by women.

The compressing of the feet of girls with tight bandages (as formerly in China) so as to keep the feet from being over three or four inches long]—Merriam-Webster Dictionary.

Take ancient China as an example. Here, women were viewed as inferior to men and were compelled to live by the 'Three Obediences': daughters must obey their fathers, wives must obey their husbands, and widows must obey their sons. It is clear that this cultural rule favored male superiority. This is but one of many examples of how societies viewed the degradation of women as acceptable. This is why we are being directed back to Eden so that we can uproot this type of ideology and learn to walk in authority alongside our male counterparts.

Around the 10th century, Chinese women subjected themselves to excruciating pain through a practice known as "foot binding[10]" This practice involved tightly binding the feet to prevent growth, as large feet were not considered beautiful. This painful custom led to limited mobility and permanent physical impairment. Despite causing immense suffering, having bound feet was regarded as a high honor for women.

> In a culture that idolizes sons and dreads the birth of a daughter, to be born female comes perilously close to being born less than human," the Indian government conceded in a recent report by its Department of Women and Child Development.
> (The Washington Post) —Born Oppressed, **John Ward Anderson** and **Molly Moore** February 14, 1993

These injustices pale in comparison to the horrors inflicted upon women in Asia, India, and South Africa. In India, having a baby boy was considered honorable, while baby girls were often killed at birth, a reflection of cultural beliefs. India's Department of Women and Child Development shockingly stated that being born a woman in India equates to being born less than human.

In countries like South Africa and Asia, women faced the constant threat of infanticide. *(being killed within a year of birth)* Girls who survived infancy endured lives marked by degradation, overwork, and malnourishment. They are often denied education, forced into marriages, prostitution, and slave labor. When a husband dies without leaving an inheritance, the wife is left homeless and forced to beg.

As I journey through these pages, what initially appeared as a message of empowerment for women has transformed into a battle cry. I am outraged

---

10 Foot binding, cultural practice, existing in China from the 10th century until the establishment of the Peoples Republic of China in 1949, that involved tightly bandaging the feet of women to alter their shape for aesthetic purposes.

by the infringement on women's God-given rights, perpetrated not by mere mortals, but by an ancient adversary—Satan himself.

How can we possibly defeat such a formidable opponent? Is victory even attainable? And if so, where do we begin?

Before we answer these questions, let's examine the dynamics of our struggles in the United States. One of the most significant threats to freedom is our willingness to accept injustice. Here in America, we often embrace elements that degrade and demean our identities, glorifying them and making them the foundation of our beauty. By doing so, we inadvertently grant the enemy rest as we destroy our self-image. Consider the ancient Chinese practice of "foot binding," which deformed women's feet in the name of beauty. These women exchanged comfort for pain to be accepted within their cultural norms. These practices were enforced from birth, leaving women with few alternatives and limited freedoms.

However, in America, a country that proudly upholds the motto of freedom, millions of women wake up daily in a state of bondage. Despite our privileges of freedom, finding true freedom within ourselves often proves challenging. Like the women in China and India, many women in America also subject themselves to painful practices in a quest for acceptance.

A clear example is the common view of women mainly as objects of sexual desire. The pursuit of an idealized body image drives numerous women to drastic actions, desperate to meet society's standards of the 'perfect' body. The trend of undergoing major surgical procedures, such as breast or buttock enhancements, is alarmingly common. In recent times, there's been a surge in confessions from women who have resorted to black-market procedures for body modifications. Alarmingly, the rate of fatalities linked to procedures like the Brazilian Butt Lift (BBL) is escalating.

Yet the relentless pressure for women to conform to rigid standards of performance and appearance persists unchanged. Thus, achieving and maintaining genuine freedom requires each of us to embark on a journey of self-discovery and transformation.

Our quest for equality begins with the reconditioning of our minds. This entails not only embracing change but also accepting the discomfort that accompanies it. We must prepare ourselves for the inevitable disruptions such change will bring into our lives, which will vary uniquely from person to person. For some, it may involve challenging and reshaping long-held cultural beliefs; for others, a shift in political and religious views might be necessary.

Moreover, for many of us, this journey will mean learning to live without the validation and affirmation we often seek from others. For some, it will involve debunking the false narratives we have created about ourselves based on gender bias. And for others, it may require challenging our commitment to laws that perpetuate injustices against women. Whatever the case, it is only through such individual awakenings that we can collectively stride towards a future where true equality prevails, and the full power and authority that women embody can be unleashed.

Our Battle Against Legislative Inequality

Moreover, these injustices against women manifest through unjust laws and legislation. For instance, although slavery was abolished in 1865, and by 1870 the 15th Amendment granted freedmen[11] the legal right to vote, Our fight for a documented right to vote proved more challenging.

While freedmen had to contend for the practical realization of their rights, it was officially documented that they deserved the right to vote. Women, however, faced the dual challenge of not only fighting for the right to vote but also battling to shift societal perceptions regarding the fundamental injustice of their disqualification. From the 19th to the 20th century, women valiantly led the suffrage movement, enduring hatred, betrayal, and intense opposition from both men and women. Their fight was for more than the right to vote; it was a crusade against inequality, a fervent plea for recognition and respect as every human being has the right to receive.

A perfect example of the relentless fight for equality is Sojourner Truth's iconic "Ain't I A Woman" speech, delivered at the Women's Convention in Akron, Ohio, in 1851. While some may whimsically reenact her speech, emphasizing her unconventional grammar, they often overlook the profound essence of her message. It was not merely a speech; it was a powerful battle cry from a woman who had validated her strength and recognized her intrinsic worth. Truth's declaration was an affirmation of her resilience, a testament to the inherent power of a woman to lead, conquer, and assert dominion. For that, she stood bold and strong, and for that reason, she established her own worth.

She epitomizes a woman in authority, choosing to be who God said she could be. Through this truth, she confronted laws and societal norms that suggested anything differently. My dear sister, what will be your

[11] Freedmen: refers to former slaves who have been released from slavery.

declaration of freedom? Have you thought about it? Are you willing to proclaim it, stand on it, and rule in it? —It's time!

Our Battle Against Religious Injustices

"These people draw near to Me with their mouth, And honor Me with their lips, But their heart is far from Me. And in vain they worship Me, Teaching as doctrines the commandments of men." -Matthew 15:8

Religion has also played a significant role in perpetuating the war on women's equality and fundamental human rights. Religious organizations have employed brutal misinterpretations of scripture to manipulate, control, and constrain women. They have enforced unquestionable submission, promoting the notion that men are superior to women in every aspect. This demands women's subservience and binds us to the ancient lie that "we were not good enough as God had created us." What a story we have lived! What a victory we have yet to win! I am ready. Are you?

Traditionally, men were the ones permitted to occupy pulpits and lead congregations in most religious institutions. Laws and traditions compelling women to submit to this absurd hierarchy primarily benefited the male leaders. Submission often meant silence or expulsion, and consequently, the church became a breeding ground for injustices against women.

Abuses carried out by tyrant church leaders have no age limits. Armed with scripture—though misinterpreted—and backed by legal and religious systems and laws, male pastors have subjected women and girls to unspeakable horrors. Girls are often taught to be silent and obedient, leaving little room for reported abuse.

In my observations, there have been instances where pastors, under the pretext of offering counseling, have conducted private meetings with young women. Tragically, it later emerged that these interactions were far from innocent.

These young girls, vulnerable and unsuspecting, were groomed and coerced into sexual encounters with their spiritual leaders. What amplifies this tragedy is the implicit trust and unquestioning submission that many parents, both mothers and fathers, placed in these leaders. This blind allegiance often led to a failure to scrutinize the leaders' actions, allowing a cycle of abuse to continue unchecked and may even extend into the victims' adult lives.

These abuses often left women estranged from a genuine relationship with God. In most instances, if they ever mustered up the strength to leave the church they would never return. For this reason, my heart sinks with exhaustion, and my tears are wet with a fervent cry for God to turn these tables of injustice and to rend the hearts of these abusers until repentance comes and then revival.

It may be difficult to face this hard truth, but many of these abuses continue to occur today. Countless women harbor painful testimonies of their experiences with church leaders. These acts are driven by satanic influences and must be confronted and dismantled in every generation to expose the enemy and set women free from the bondage of the fall.

We Are Prevailing

Despite these adversities, God's daughters have persevered and prevailed. In recent years, more women have risen to leadership within religious institutions, asserting their right to share the wisdom God has bestowed upon them. The act of preaching, although accepted, is still met with significant opposition. The magnitude of our mantle often strikes fear in our male counterparts. The result is often the same: carrying the weight of mockery and being marginalized. Yet, we are standing strong and overcoming these challenges like true warriors.

In the early 1990s, Bishop T.D. Jakes launched a movement called "Woman Thou Art Loosed" declaring freedom from bondage, guilt, and shame for women. He preached breakthrough and deliverance, and women worldwide pressed their way into his meeting places. They postured themselves in expectation, waiting to hear a word of liberation and freedom. Women waited eagerly to undergo the transforming power of Bishop Jake's words.

This single message of hope and inspiration woke women up everywhere and freed them from the bands of their captors. I was certainly one who basked in its ray of hope. Indeed, I take nothing from this great man of God, whose mantle has been proven.

However, I am afraid that being loosed wasn't nearly enough, and that what Bishop Jakes offered was only a small step towards the recovery of the Lady Kings' crown. Bishop Jakes proclaimed our freedom and negotiated our release. However, being released does not guarantee complete freedom. I believe this movement has led us to a mountain, and just like the children of Israel, we have been wandering there for years. We profess freedom but embrace bondage. However, if we are to walk in total freedom, we must command it ourselves. Trust me, ladies, we know power, but we must become acquainted with authority. We have the right and ability to free ourselves from the bondage of the fall.

Women have been in captivity to the bondage of the fall since the beginning of time. Although we are physically released, we often remain mentally attached. Because of this, I believe we are entering a new movement on the same scale, perhaps even greater than the one Bishop Jakes initiated.

This new transition will bring a breakthrough and will free us from our wilderness wandering. We need a fresh wind to shift us away from the politics of freedom and into the heart of advancement. We must be free enough to possess the mountain of equality and overthrow the injustice of exclusion. Freedom starts in the mind, and once your mind is renewed, the movement becomes second nature.

What does this mean for us? It signifies that in this season, women everywhere will undergo another awakening. This awakening will unveil our true identity—we are kings. Once our crowns have been recovered, we will rule with confidence. The shackles of defeat will be shattered from our minds. We will no longer dance to the beat of the enemy's drums, nor will we bow to the sound of his trumpet. Thus, we are free and so shall we act as a freed nation of people.

Once our minds are liberated, we will reclaim our rightful position. As a result, our Man-Kings will acknowledge us once again, proclaiming, "This is flesh of my flesh and bone of my bone—a power equal to mine!" We will overcome rejection, self-hate, abuse, mental disturbances, alcoholism, promiscuity, jealousy, witchcraft, and Jezebel spirits, among others.

We have indeed come a long way! Yet, we find ourselves still engaged in a relentless battle, and we must remain vigilant in this season as we embark upon a new movement. Achieving momentum in areas dominated by tyranny will not be a simple feat. And you might find that the most challenging adversary to convince of your rightful status as a Lady King is yourself.

Furthermore, you are likely to face considerable opposition from the wounded Lady Kings you encounter on your journey. These are the sisters who have not yet experienced healing and restoration. Your engagement with them will need to be multifaceted: not only must you fend off their attempts to derail your progress, but you must also wage a spiritual battle for the liberation of their minds from the enemy's grasp.

Yet, in this endeavor, be assured that God will fortify and empower you, for the victory of our redemption is a source of immense joy to Him. The road ahead may be fraught with challenges, but we are called to advance, empowered by His strength, as we claim the victory that is already ours. Let us move forward with confidence, knowing that in His pleasure lies our ultimate victory.

May you recover your mantle with the grace and dignity that only a Lady King possesses.

____

Highlights of A Lady King

04: The Fight to Recover | Melinda Gates

Philanthropist, Business Women & Writer (August 1964)

"When we invest in women and girls, we are investing in the people who invest in everyone else."—Melinda Gates

Melinda Gates, born Melinda Ann French on August 15, 1964, in Dallas, Texas, is a prominent American philanthropist, businesswoman, and writer. She graduated from Duke University with a degree in computer science and economics and began her career as a marketing manager at Microsoft Corporation. It was at Microsoft where she met Bill Gates, co-founder of the company, and whom she later married.

Her most notable contribution is co-founding and co-chairing the Bill & Melinda Gates Foundation, the world's largest private charitable foundation. The foundation, established in 2000, focuses on addressing global issues like health, education, and poverty. It operates in three primary divisions: global health, global development, and community and education causes in the United States.

Melinda Gates is also recognized for her advocacy for women's equality and empowerment. In addition to her work with the foundation, she founded Pivotal Ventures, an investment and incubation company that aims to advance social progress for women and families in the United States.

Her influence and impact have been widely acknowledged, with Forbes magazine consistently ranking her as one of the world's most powerful women. This acknowledgment stems not just from her philanthropic efforts but also from her role as a global advocate for women and girls.

Melinda Gates' life and work exemplify a commitment to improving global health, alleviating poverty, and empowering women and girls, making her a leading figure in philanthropy and social advocacy.

Biblical Example

Jael(Judges 4:17-22)

In the biblical narrative found in Judges 4:17-22, Jael emerges as a pivotal and courageous figure. Her actions significantly contributed to the victory of Israel over the Canaanite army, led by their commander Sisera.

The story unfolds as Sisera flees the battlefield after a crushing defeat by the Israelite forces under the leadership of Deborah and Barak. Seeking refuge, he arrives at the tent of Jael, who belongs to the Kenite tribe, a group neutral in the conflict between Israel and Canaan. Despite this neutrality, Jael's actions suggest a covert allegiance to the Israelite cause.

Jael welcomes Sisera into her tent, offering him sanctuary and comfort. This act of hospitality initially seems to provide Sisera with a safe haven. However, Jael's intentions are far from benign. Once Sisera is asleep, Jael seizes the opportunity to strike a decisive blow for Israel. She takes a tent peg and a hammer and, demonstrating both bravery and decisiveness, drives the peg through Sisera's temple, killing him instantly. This act of lethal determination not only eliminates the Canaanite commander but also signifies a turning point in the struggle, leading to the eventual triumph of the Israelites over their oppressors.

Jael's actions, while violent, are portrayed as an act of divine intervention. The biblical text suggests that her deed was part of a larger, divinely orchestrated plan to deliver Israel from its enemies. This perspective is further reinforced in the Song of Deborah, found in Judges 5, which celebrates Jael's deed and extols her as a heroine of Israel.

This truth is our foundation as we confront internal struggles and maintain our integrity in the face of opposition, even when it comes from another 'Lady King'. Though challenging, we must stand firm, unwavering in the face of opposition, whether it emanates from external sources or from within ourselves."

Photo Credit: **Rich Allela** and **Dapel Kureng**

Chapter 05

Unmasking the Wounded Lady King

Shall I bring to the time of birth, and not cause delivery?" says the Lord. "Shall I who cause delivery shut up the womb?" says your God.
-Isaiah 66:9NKJV

Merriam-Webster Dictionary: *Defines "wounded" as being injured, hurt by, or suffering from a wound. This can refer to a physical injury like a wounded leg, as well as emotional suffering, as in wounded feelings.*

Equality for women has been pursued from one decade to another. Renowned women from past ages have stood at the forefront, pleading for justice, and at times demanding it. Similarly, many 'Lady Kings' are wide awake in this season, prepared for battle. Although the opposition has not ceased, we have remained diligent in our pursuit of equality for women. Yet, our adversary has not relented. In fact, his tactics have become increasingly volatile, utilizing internal wounds to slow the progression of our freedom. However, God has assured us that He will not bring us to the brink of delivery without ensuring that we give birth.

Therefore, this chapter is dedicated to healing the wounds that may impair our ability to walk in total freedom. We will explore four major areas of internal struggles: Inadequacy, Jealousy, Inward Bondage, and

Weariness. We will consider how these internal struggles might become hindrances to our freedom.

In the pages ahead, we will focus on ways to unmask these wounds. This includes examining how we can achieve personal freedom from each one. We will also explore strategies for dealing with a fellow 'Lady King' who may be oppressed by these same internal struggles and learn how to navigate the potential onslaught of attacks that may result from them.

> Always engage the battle with her face to face; pray confront, forgive and pray. But don't ever succumb to malicious backbiting and slandering of your sister.

It is crucial to understand that opposition will inevitably arise. However, we must hold fast to God's promise—He will not bring us to the time of birth without ensuring that we deliver. This truth is our foundation as we confront internal struggles and maintain our integrity in the face of opposition, even when it comes from another 'Lady King'. Though challenging, we must stand firm and unwavering in the face of opposition, whether it comes from external sources or from within ourselves.

In the following paragraphs, I will describe several reasons why one woman may oppose another as both pursue equality and victory. As you read through this section take an intense look in the mirror. Ask God if any of these issues are found in you. If so, repent and move forward. Furthermore, if you find yourself in a situation where your sister is opposing you, remember this guiding principle for every battle you may face with her: Always engage in the battle face to face. Pray, confront, forgive, and pray again. But never succumb to malicious backbiting and slandering of your sister (James 4:11). Let your confrontations be conducted in love and for the purpose of upholding Kingdom principles (Matthew 18:15-17).

This type of confrontation is healthy and biblical. In Galatians 2:11-13, the Apostle Paul confronted Peter face to face when he found an issue with him. Ironically, leaving these issues unspoken could have caused a major division amongst the group and perhaps may have even hindered the progression of Kingdom movements. In Matthew 18:15-17 we are encouraged to follow this example to quickly resolve issues that may arise amongst us

Neglecting to engage in healthy confrontation only serves to empower the enemy's tactics against both you and your sister in Christ. The foremost goal in these situations should always be mutual deliverance and healing. Confronting real issues, though it may be uncomfortable, is essential. It's a process of bringing every matter into the divine light of God's love and trusting in His power to bring about healing and resolution.

Similarly, it is vital to trust God to reveal any internal wounds that may be lingering within you. Facing these internal challenges can be daunting, but it is crucial to address them head-on, no matter how uncomfortable it may feel. This act of bravery is not just for your own spiritual health but also for the health of the entire community of believers. By confronting these issues, both externally and internally, you allow God's healing power to work not only in your life but also in the lives of those around you.

Buckle up and let's take a close look in the mirror!

Unmasking the Opposition of Inadequacy

Definition: "A feeling of inadequacy, lack of self-confidence, and inability to cope, accompanied by general uncertainty and anxiety about one's goals, abilities, or relationships with others. (American Psychological Association, (n.d.)

Satan often imposes this pattern of thinking on many unsuspecting women, silently whispering to them that they lack something vital that prevents them from walking in purpose. Although this assumption is devoid of truth, it is a masterful tactic used to shift the mindset of a woman away from her God-given purpose as a daughter and ruling Lady King on Earth.

This attack is most potent in the private corridors of the mind. It is there that the enemy plants small seeds of insecurity, doubt, unworthiness, and despair. This combination is a recipe for disaster as it affects not only the individual having these thoughts but also obstructs relationships, friendships, partnerships, divine collaborations, and so much more, making it impossible for the woman who is experiencing this opposition to receive freedom for herself or be able to offer it to someone else.

A woman dealing with feelings of inadequacy often exhibits distinctive traits and behaviors that reflect the inner turmoil that holds her hostage. Below are some detailed characteristics:

- **Persistent Search for Validation:** Constantly seeks external validation and affirmation, believing that she needs approval from others to feel accomplished.
- **Mimicry and Imitation:** Tends to imitate or mimic the actions and behaviors of others, often attempting to replicate what she perceives

as wholeness or validation in someone else.

- **Frequent Feelings of Frustration:** Experiences frustration regularly, especially when her attempts to mimic others or seek external validation fall short, leading to a cycle of discouragement.
- **Difficulty Maintaining Healthy Friendships:** Struggles to maintain long-lasting, healthy friendships due to the constant fear of being exposed as inadequate. This fear hinders her ability to connect genuinely with others.
- **Negative Outlook and Criticism:** Adopts a negative outlook on various aspects of life, including herself and others. Often critical of situations and people, finding fault even where it may not exist.
- **Fear of Exposure and Rejection**: Carries a deep-seated fear of being exposed as incomplete or inadequate. This fear of exposure makes it challenging for her to remain in one place or maintain relationships for an extended period, fearing eventual rejection.
- **Pattern of Sabotage:** Unconsciously engages in self-sabotaging behaviors, especially when faced with challenges or setbacks. This pattern of sabotage may manifest as a defense mechanism against the perceived threat of exposure.
- **Constant Need for Reassurance:** Frequently seeks reassurance from others, pleading for attention and affirmation. In moments of perceived neglect, she may accuse others of insensitivity, desperately craving acknowledgment and validation.
- **Identity Crisis and Lack of Confidence:** Struggles with a sense of identity, often feeling lost and unsure of her purpose. Lacks confidence in her own abilities and may attempt to compensate by adopting the characteristics of others.
- **Tendency to Project Inadequacy:** Projects her feelings of inadequacy onto others by being negative about everything and everyone. This projection is a defense mechanism to divert attention

from her own perceived shortcomings.

Recognizing Inadequacy Within

The feeling of being inadequate forces a person into isolation. Often, the thoughts, reactions, and even feelings that you may harbor towards another woman are a projection of a negative self-perception. This mental state fosters its own little torture chamber inside your mind, perpetuating a constant state of bondage with all its overpowering nudges and suggestions.

However, if you are enduring this battle, there is hope for freedom, but it will require stepping beyond your comfort zone. In doing so there are three steps that you must take toward freedom:

Step One - Honesty: Admit the truth about your thoughts and the tremendous amount of agony they have caused you. Do this first in prayer, admitting to God that your feelings of inadequacy have left you at a disadvantage for freedom. Then, ask God to show you whom, how, and where to trust this information. By confessing this truth to your fellow sister in Christ, a breakthrough, and the freedom to be the Lady King that God called you to be will suddenly emerge.

As James 5:16 states, "Confess your faults one to another, and pray one for another, that ye may be healed. The effectual fervent prayer of a righteous man availeth much." (KJV)

Step Two - Ask for Help: Once you have acknowledged this emotion, you must be willing to ask for and accept help. Understand that help doesn't always look the way we imagine. The help you need may come from a person you are currently rejecting.

As Isaiah 55:8-9 declares, "For my thoughts are not your thoughts, neither are your ways my ways," declares the LORD. "As the heavens are higher than the earth, so are my ways higher than your ways and my thoughts than your thoughts."

Step Three - Oppose Negative Thoughts: The enemy is relentless in his pursuit of you; therefore, he will never cease presenting alternative, negative thoughts. These thoughts seek to mask the true will and purpose of God for your life. They will not stop because you ignore them, but they will surrender defeated because you opposed them. Therefore, you must take a militant stand against negative thoughts, allowing the Holy Spirit to guide you in the truth of your identity.

"Submit yourselves therefore to God. Resist the devil, and he will flee from you." James 4:7

Encountering & Dealing With Inadequacy

Before assisting your fellow sister in Christ who may be struggling with feelings of inadequacy, it's crucial to conduct a self-evaluation to ensure you're not facing the same oppression. Once you've completed your spiritual check, consider these steps to help your fellow sister in Christ overcome the opposition of inadequacy.

Empathy and Mercy: Recall your battles with this oppressive spirit and approach her situation with empathy and mercy.

Healthy Confrontation: Engage in direct, face-to-face conversations. Be honest about the emotional attacks from the enemy. Guide her in recognizing that she may perceive things negatively due to the spirit of inadequacy influencing her to be judgmental, condescending, and difficult.

Understand Her Challenges: Recognize that her fear of exposure, stemming from feelings of not being good enough, may lead her to avoid transparency and, consequently, cause difficulties for her in maintaining long-term connections.

Avoid Misalignment: While trying to help, be cautious not to lose sight of your purpose and vision. Continuous attempts to understand her issues without resolution can lead to dead ends. Listen for the Holy Spirit's guidance as to when to pull back for a moment. Remember wounds take time to heal and taking a mental break is often a part of the process.

Prayer and Contention: Confronting the oppressive spirit of inadequacy in your sister may lead to contention. If you confront her and it leads to a negative reaction, be prepared to support her through prayer. Asking God to keep the peace between you and her.

Keep in mind that we all struggle with something, therefore even if this portion was not your struggle you should still be eager to empathize with a clear understanding of what it feels like to be oppressed by an inward struggle Remember to be patient, but direct and kind. And when it's time to let go or if you must let go do so in love.

Unmasking The Opposition of Jealousy

Jealousy: a feeling of unhappiness and anger because someone has something or someone that you want. - Cambridge Dictionary

One of the most challenging and volatile oppositions many women face is the persistent spirit of jealousy. Ironically, this emotion is often fueled by feelings of inadequacy. Jealousy serves as a silent adversary, quietly residing in the heart, intertwining with every emotion. It causes the "wounded lady king" to suffer in silence, breeding mountains of insecurity. Proverbs 27:4 (NKJV) aptly describes the destructive power of jealousy:

> "Wrath is cruel and anger a torrent, but who is able to stand before jealousy?"—Proverbs 27:4 (NKJV)

The wound of jealousy can penetrate deeply within us, especially when we find ourselves merely imitating the freedom that our identity in Christ should bring, rather than truly receiving and embracing it. Recognizing this form of spiritual bondage is crucial. Several key indicators can help you determine if you are in bondage to the invasive spirit of jealousy.

Intrusive Thoughts: The onset of jealousy can be very subtle, as small thoughts about another sister in Christ invade your mind. They often come uninvited and linger if allowed. Though initially undetected by others, these thoughts can feel so potent that it seems as if the person can see them.

Overly Flattering: In an attempt to suppress these evasive thoughts, you might overly flatter the individual(s) toward whom these feelings are directed, sometimes even diminishing your own worth in comparison.

Taking on False Burdens: To prove to yourself that you are not jealous, you might make commitments to that person that are overwhelming and unrealistic for you to manage.

Instability: In extreme cases, overwhelming feelings of jealousy can cause you to pull away without explanation.

Love/Hate Relationships: It's common to genuinely care for the person who triggers feelings of jealousy. You might find yourself earnestly praying for and supporting their success, yet their achievements can paradoxically intensify your jealousy. This is a cruel attack from the enemy that, if unaddressed, will only fester and worsen.

Inability to Celebrate Others: When jealousy takes root, it becomes challenging to genuinely celebrate your fellow sister's success, as it triggers feelings of inadequacy and low self-esteem. This sabotage may manifest as emotional breakdowns during celebratory moments, distancing without explanation, and eventually evolving into judgment and negativity.

Recognizing Jealousy Within

Admitting feelings of jealousy can be challenging due to the associated sense of shame, leading to embarrassment about even experiencing such emotions. Those oppressed by this spirit often allow it to fester for extended periods.

I believe that every woman will, at some point, experience jealousy or envy. The depth of its influence is determined by how one handles this fierce emotion when it arises.

Interestingly, shame arises from feelings of inadequacy, and admitting to jealousy can feel like an acknowledgment that someone else is better or has something more valuable. This admission triggers further feelings of inadequacy and a cascade of emotions such as guilt and even depression. Jealousy's unexpected appearance often leaves individuals feeling caught off guard, ashamed, and guilty about their feelings.

I believe that every woman will, at some point, experience jealousy or envy. The depth of its influence is determined by how one handles this fierce emotion when it arises. Recognizing jealousy within yourself at its onset is key. Observe your reactions to a peer's success or aspirations. Do you feel inadequate, or do you find yourself comparing your achievements to hers? These feelings often manifest subtly, leading to overcompensation through excessive praise or unsolicited advice. While compliments and assistance are valuable, they must come from a place of sincerity. If your actions don't align with your heart, take a moment to confront and renounce jealousy. Refuse to let it dwell in your mind. True lady kings, secure in their identity, do not need to covet what others have.

Encountering & Dealing With Jealousy

Jealousy can manifest among sisters, striking at any moment. It often springs from low self-esteem, stemming from the wounded Lady King's loss of identity. What makes it particularly deceptive is its concealment; it operates within the heart, hidden from plain sight.

Jealousy can escalate into envy and, if left unchecked, lead to bitterness and resentment. Jealousy brings with it a host of negative traits. James 3:16 states that where envy and strife exist, all kinds of negative actions emerge.

Those ensnared by this spirit often become suspicious of everyone, even those without ill intentions. Their skewed perception creates a sense that everyone harbors harmful intentions towards them.

When you encounter another sister wrestling with jealousy towards you, she may strive to resist its harmful pull at first. Even so, small signs will alert you that something is wrong. It's important to note mentally that the battle for her is internal and overwhelming—be kind. However, be aware and alert that the internal battle also carries depth and often explores the darkest corridors of the mind. When jealousy is present, every evil thought can occur, unfortunately, directed squarely at you. If this spirit is not exposed and cast out, the oppressed person may find themselves wishing and praying for your demise or even bringing false accusations against you based on their own skewed perception.

A biblical example of such jealousy can be found in the story of Mary and Martha. When Jesus visited their home, Martha's jealousy toward her sister, Mary, was evident as she questioned Mary's role and assignment.

> *Now it came to pass, as they went, that he entered into a certain village: and a certain woman named Martha received him into her house. And she had a sister called Mary, which also sat at Jesus' feet, and heard his word. But Martha was burdened about much serving, and came to him, and said, Lord, dost thou not care that my sister hath left me to serve alone? Bid her therefore that she help me." (Luke 10:38-42, KJV)*

Mary and Martha were likely at different stages of maturity. Martha was engrossed in the tasks of preparation, possibly considering service as her gift to the Messiah. In contrast, Mary had reached a deeper level of maturity. She understood that, while work was essential, the Messiah's presence took precedence over any labor. Her growth as a mature Lady King had taught her that the most crucial aspect was spending time in His presence. Mature Lady Kings comprehend that successful Kingdom ministry stems from an intimate relationship with the Father.

The story of King Saul's relationship with David serves as another biblical example. Although David had no intention of usurping King Saul's throne, Saul's jealousy of David's anointing consumed him. After David's victory over the Philistines, Saul's jealousy turned to rage. Throughout his life, Saul made numerous attempts to assassinate David because of his jealousy. *(1 Samuel 18:10-11, 1 Samuel 19:1,1 Samuel 19:9-10)*

When jealousy takes hold of a woman, she may attempt to mask it with insincere flattery, hoping to compensate for her underlying resentment. However, witnessing another Lady King's progress in ministry can trigger intense jealousy, causing her to withdraw to avoid arousing her resentful feelings. Surprisingly, the more recognition her sister receives, the fiercer her jealousy burns.

This individual can inadvertently harm your ministry, family, or employment, causing others to question your integrity as a woman of God. If your sister struggles with jealousy, approach her with compassion, recalling your own experiences with these feelings. Extend grace and space for her growth. Seek God's guidance on how to assist her in breaking free from jealousy.

However, if jealousy has evolved into bitterness, anger, and hatred, it may be necessary to distance yourself from the situation. If your sister is willing to seek help, connect her with someone who can guide her towards deliverance. If she refuses assistance, disconnect from her in love, interceding on her behalf as prompted by the Holy Spirit

Unmasking Inward Bondage

"It is for freedom that Christ has set us free. Stand firm, then, and do not let yourselves be burdened again by a yoke of slavery."—Galalations 5:1

Inward bondage often refers to a state where an individual is internally constrained or restricted by emotional, psychological, or spiritual factors.

We are constantly faced with struggles as we strive to accept and embrace our true identity in Christ, for both ourselves and others. However, along the way, we may occasionally encounter a sister-friend who, at first glance, seems to personify freedom. Yet, a closer examination may reveal her struggle with inward bondage despite an outward projection of liberty. Subtle remnants of her past life serve as a stark reminder of her ongoing battle for true freedom in Christ Jesus. Inward bondage can manifest in a variety of ways, some of which are listed below:

- **False Freedom:** She maintains a mask of freedom and success, skillfully concealing the emotional chains still clinging on from her past.
- **Impeccable Image:** She is deeply invested in maintaining a flawless exterior, diligently ensuring that her past doesn't resurface or reflect her previous self. This often involves a strong focus on outward appearances.
- **Charismatic Exterior:** With her charisma and a strong grasp of scripture, she assumes leadership roles and is actively involved in church life, often serving as a role model outwardly.
- **Emotional Attachment:** Despite physical freedom, she remains emotionally tied to her past struggles, with memories often haunting her, creating an unseen internal conflict.
- **Secrecy and Isolation:** Her struggles are mostly kept hidden, and seldom confided to others. This secrecy often leads to isolation, hindering the development of genuine relationships.
- **Resistance to Deliverance:** When the need for deliverance is suggested, she persistently denies its necessity, insisting on her freedom, and avoiding any transparency about her inner battles.
- **Fear of Exposure:** Haunted by the fear of her true self and past being exposed, she is compelled to maintain her mask, allowing this fear to significantly influence her actions and decisions.
- **Control Mechanisms:** Driven by a need to control her image, her insecurity manifests in behaviors like constantly striving to out perform others or using manipulation to avoid rejection.

- **Self-Promotion and False Alliances**: Driven by a fear of failure, she engages in self-promotion and forms insincere or ungodly alliances, often leading to further disappointment and pain.
- **Repeated Patterns:** She is caught in a continuous loop of upholding her image, seeking unfruitful alliances, and facing disappointment and discouragement once she chooses the wrong people, a cycle that will persist until she confronts her inner turmoil.
- **Vicious Attacks to Protect Image:** When her image is threatened, she may resort to covert but aggressive tactics against those perceived as threats to her image.
- **Pattern of Disconnection:** In the face of confrontation or potential exposure, she may abruptly sever connections. However, this disconnection might not be permanent, as she may eventually re-emerge still broken and still hidden.

Encountering & Dealing With Inward Bondage

This wounded Lady King skillfully conceals her struggles beneath an image of freedom, possibly having escaped an abusive relationship, conquered addiction, or distanced herself from a chaotic past. Regardless of the narrative, she carefully crafts an impeccable image, skillfully hiding her history. Charismatic and well-versed in scripture, she often holds leadership roles, leading an active church life, garnering admiration, and serving as a role model. However, beneath the surface, she is wounded, emotionally bound to the stains of her past. Yet these struggles have become her best-kept secret.

When confronted with opposition from this Lady King, brace yourself for an intense battle. She forcefully rejects the need for deliverance, asserting she is already free. Suggestions to unveil the mask of her false identity and seek genuine deliverance are met with resistance. Transparency becomes her greatest threat as she is committed to appearing perfect.

Consider the encounter of Jesus with the Samaritan woman at the well. She, too, was in disguise, hoping to evade the discovery of her past. Yet, Jesus, with profound transparency, offered her refuge and healing.

"The woman saith unto him, Sir, I perceive that thou art a prophet. Come, see a man, which told me all things that ever I did: is not this the Christ?"

(John 4:16-19)

This wounded Lady King is fearful of not succeeding. She often resorts to self-promotion, fostering false or ungodly alliances that may not ever work out in her favor. However, the cycle will continue until she confronts the inward turmoil that holds her captive.

Connecting with this sister proves challenging as she guards herself behind a carefully constructed image. Requesting her to be open about her pain might trigger a fierce attack against you. Handling this situation requires healthy confrontation, even if it means addressing the issue multiple times.

If she chooses to disconnect, the healthiest response is to let go, refusing to validate her misguided actions. This step, while challenging, respects both her independence and your boundaries. It's important to recognize that holding on to someone who isn't ready for change can be detrimental to both parties involved.

However, should she return, it's crucial to gently yet firmly revisit the core issues. Suggest that any unresolved matters be addressed before moving forward. This approach helps to avoid repeating patterns of false deliverance and superficial healing. It's not just about reconciliation but about ensuring that the journey towards healing is genuine and rooted in truth.

By adhering to this method, you may not only regain a sister in Christ but also significantly contribute to her recovery. This process sets her on a path of dynamic kingdom-building, where her experiences become testimonies of transformation and strength.

In this delicate balance of release and welcome, remember that your role is not to force change but to facilitate an environment where true healing can occur. Your steadfastness in truth, coupled with compassion and patience, can be instrumental in guiding her back to a path of authentic freedom and restoration.

- **Start With Prayer**: Begin with prayer, both for wisdom in how to approach her and for her own healing and deliverance. Prayer lays the foundation for any spiritual battle and opens the door for God's intervention.
- **Empathetic Listening:** Show empathy and understanding without judgment. This can create an environment of trust where she may feel safe to open up about her struggles.
- **Gentle Confrontation:** When the time is right, gently confront her about the issues you perceive. This should be done in love and with the intention of helping, not condemning her. Remember, it's about restoring her, not exposing her.
- **Offer Biblical Guidance:** Use the Bible as your guide. The story of the Samaritan woman is a perfect example of how Jesus dealt with someone with a similar background. He offered her living water—a chance to be healed not judged.
- **Consistent Support**: Be prepared to offer ongoing support.

Recovery and healing from deep emotional wounds don't happen overnight.

- **Encourage Transparency and Accountability:** While respecting her privacy, encourage her to be transparent about her struggles.
- **Setting Boundaries:** If the situation becomes toxic or harmful to your spiritual health, it's important to set boundaries. This isn't about giving up on her but about protecting yourself and ensuring that the ministry environment remains healthy and safe for everyone involved.
- **Be Open to Professional Help:** Recognize when the situation is beyond your expertise. There's no shame in encouraging her to seek professional counseling or therapy.

In all of these situations, remember that your primary role is to serve as a vessel for God's love and healing power. It is ultimately God who heals and restores. Place your trust in Him to work in the lives of those around you.

However, if you recognize yourself in these descriptions, the first person you need to confront is yourself. Approach this with prayerfulness and honesty. Seek support from those who love you. Continually pray and ask God to guide your steps toward complete freedom, trusting in His divine guidance and healing.

Unmasking The Opposition of Weariness

Merriam-Webster Dictionary: Describes weariness as a state of being "exhausted in strength, endurance, vigor, or freshness," also noting that it includes the expression or characteristic of weariness and the state of having one's patience, tolerance, or pleasure exhausted.

And let us not be weary in well doing: for in due season we shall reap if we faint not.- Galatians 6:9 (KJV)

I have chosen weariness as the final opposition that wounded 'Lady Kings' experience, for several compelling reasons. Firstly, weariness is a condition that often emerges after many battles, irrespective of whether they were won or lost. It represents the cumulative toll of continuous struggle, not just the outcome of individual conflicts.

Secondly, weariness is frequently misunderstood as mere rebellion, leading to a tragic misapplication of responses. Rather than offering healing, this misperception results in the infliction of additional hurt, worsening the weariness instead of relieving it.

Lastly, in this state of weariness, what was once a powerful vessel of strength and might and a formidable force becomes passive. The individual, burdened by exhaustion, may simply retire, give up, cease to care, and refuse to move forward. This stagnation is particularly dangerous because if left unaddressed, we risk ending our journey unaccomplished and unfulfilled, despite being filled with dreams and visions. Weariness, therefore, is not just a personal struggle; it is a barrier that can prevent the realization of our full purpose and the fruition of our expected end.

Many women have encountered this profound state of weariness after years dedicated to the good fight of faith. This weariness often stems from the relentless battle to affirm self-worth, gain recognition as true agents of God, and exercise dominion and power with authority and command. Such a struggle can be daunting.

If revival does not reach these weary souls, the risk of spiritual and emotional destruction is inevitable. Therefore we must extend hope, healing, and the promise of resurrection. In the pages that follow, we will embark on this crucial endeavor, offering guidance and support to revive and empower these weary warriors of faith.

Weariness takes on a distinct set of characteristics. If you or another woman is suffering from weariness these are a few signs to watch for:

Characteristics of Weariness:

- **Exhaustion from Battle:** Long-term engagement in ministry efforts without seeing the desired change. Absent of seasons of rest and receiving an outpouring for yourself. Sometimes more dedicated to the work than private moments along with God so that He can re-fill us.
- **Loss of Faith:** Diminished belief in the effectiveness and transformative power of ministry. The strain of the battles becomes overwhelming and the constant attacks from the kingdom of darkness may have you question the purpose of your faith and commitment to Kingdom Advancement.
- **Deep Wounds:** Emotional scars from standing firm in faith, often in solitary defiance.
- **Victimization:** Suffering under tyrannical leadership, and facing manipulation and jealousy may leave you feeling victimized by everyone.
- **Disdain for Institutional Church:** A sense of betrayal leading to skepticism of church practices and leaders.
- **Flickers of Hope:** Despite weariness, an occasional glimmer of hope for a pure-hearted ministry that preaches and lives the Kingdom of God remains.

Encountering & Dealing With Weariness

This Lady King is not opposed to you or your ministry; she's simply weary. Her fatigue has led her to doubt the potential for change in people's lives.

Her wounds run deep, and she's often been the steadfast one when others wavered.

Her journey has been marred by encounters with tyrant leaders, marked by inconsistency, and tainted by jealousy. She's submitted, only to be taken advantage of. Her experiences have left her with a profound disdain for the institutional church and its various elements. She views it with skepticism, feeling that it sometimes falls short of reflecting God's true nature. Despite her efforts to restrain her discontent, moments of reflection can reveal her frustrations, especially when she recalls her attempts to implement her vision without the support of fellow Lady Kings.

> Restoring this wounded Lady King requires personal investment. Encourage her to rekindle her faith in this season of restoration for women.

Should you encounter this Lady King on your journey, it's crucial to recognize her sense of abandonment and misuse. At one point, she poured her heart and soul into ministry, but repeated letdowns from pastors, lay members, friends, and even family have left her disheartened. She may appear weary, but a flicker of determination still burns within her. Occasionally, she may secretly yearn for ministry to operate from a place of purity, with a sole focus on the Kingdom of God.

However, if you fail to acknowledge her struggle, she may unintentionally discourage you. Before long, both of you may find yourselves disheartened, trapped in a state of retreat. While discouraging you is not her intention, your retreat may confirm her belief that ministry is ineffective and that achieving women's equality is an insurmountable challenge.

Restoring this wounded Lady King requires personal investment. Encourage her to rekindle her faith in this season of restoration for women. Remind her that God can transform her ashes into beauty. Challenge her to rise once more, directing her towards those who hunger and thirst for Christ. With patience and support, you may witness the spark of glory reignite in her eyes.

Weariness, though a formidable adversary, is not an insurmountable one. Once identified, its grip can be loosened, allowing progression in one's mandate, gifts, and calling to resume. For those who find themselves in the clutches of weariness, remember:

- **Seek Help Aggressively:** Don't hesitate to admit when you've reached your limits. Like Moses, who needed Joshua to support his arms, you too may need someone to help you in your time of need.
- **Declare a Time of Rest:** Actively seek a renewed outpouring from God. Immerse yourself in His Word to rebuild your strength. Let this be a season of receiving, not giving. Rest until you tangibly feel your strength returning.
- **Evaluate Your Core Group:** Examine your immediate circle. Are there individuals who can replenish your spirit? If your circle consists solely of those who draw from you, pray for God to bring into your life those who can fortify and support you.
- **Be Open to a New Move:** Embrace the possibility of a significant shift. Weariness might signal a time to explore new territories, welcome new relationships, or receive fresh visions from God.
- **Let Go When Necessary:** Be ready to conclude assignments or relationships that have run their course. Recognizing the end of a phase is crucial. Lingering too long can be a symptom of perfectionism, a cycle that can cause weariness and hinder growth.

As reiterated throughout this book, addressing your own challenges is pivotal before aiding others. Once you have personally overcome weariness, you'll be better equipped to recognize and alleviate it in others. To do so effectively, consider the following steps:

- **Be Gentle:** Approach this weary soul with gentleness. Acknowledge the numerous battles she has fought and won. Listen attentively to her struggles, without hastening her return to ministry, irrespective of her anointing or gifts.
- **Give Honor:** If she is a true vessel of God, bestow upon her double honor. Recognize and respect her mandate and anointing, and be careful not to diminish her worth due to her current state.
- **Listen Intently:** Her story may seem repetitive, but listen earnestly. In her words, you may discover where she 'lost her ax head,' akin to the story of Elijah and Elisha. This understanding will be crucial to her recovery.
- **Pour Into Her:** Understand that she currently lacks the strength to revive herself. It's your turn to shower her with love, compassion, prayer, and the warmth of your embrace.
- **Stand With Her:** As she prepares to re-enter her calling with renewed strength, offer your unwavering support. Collaborate with her in ministry where possible, affirm her visions and insights, and accompany her as she ventures into new territories and embarks on fresh endeavors in ministry and life.

In confronting weariness, these steps are not merely strategies; they are acts of spiritual wisdom. They are meant to be a guide to help you and those you minister to be free. Mingle them with prayer and allow the Holy Spirit to guide you. –I speak from experience and wisdom that only comes from God.—Selah

Finally, my sisters, shake yourselves, for God is returning your crown. Renounce the things of the past that may have caused you to fight against another Lady King. For surely, in this hour, we have work to do. God has brought us to the point of delivery! Shall we not give birth?"— Selah

Highlights of A Lady King

05: Unmasking The Wounded Lady King | Rosa Parks Civil Rights Advocate | (February 1913-October 2005)

"You must never be fearful about what you are doing when it is right."—Rosa Parks

Rosa Parks, born on February 4, 1913, in Tuskegee, Alabama, and passing away on October 24, 2005, in Detroit, Michigan, is renowned as a pivotal figure in the American Civil Rights Movement. Her act of defiance on December 1, 1955, when she refused to give up her seat on a segregated bus in Montgomery, Alabama, sparked the Montgomery Bus Boycott. This event is considered a critical moment that ignited the civil rights movement in the United States.

Parks was raised in an environment where the Ku Klux Klan was a constant threat, and she experienced racism in various forms from an early age. Despite these challenges, she became actively involved in the civil rights movement. Before her historic act on the bus, Parks was already an accomplished activist. She worked with the NAACP on several civil rights cases, including the Scottsboro Boys case. Contrary to popular simplification, Parks' refusal to give up her seat was not because she was physically tired but was a deliberate act of protest against unfair treatment.

Following her act of defiance, Parks faced arrest and a court trial. Her case garnered national attention and led to a city-wide boycott of Montgomery buses by African Americans, severely impacting the bus company's revenue. The boycott, which lasted 381 days, was a significant action against segregation, and it led to the U.S. Supreme Court's decision to declare Montgomery's segregated bus seating unconstitutional. Parks' courage and resolve in standing up against racial injustice earned her the title "mother of the civil rights movement".

After the boycott, Parks continued her activism, moving to Detroit and working for Congressman John Conyers, Jr. She co-founded the Rosa and Raymond Parks Institute for Self-Development, which aimed to provide career training for young people and educate them about the civil rights movement. Parks received numerous awards, including the Presidential Medal of Freedom and the Congressional Gold Medal. Her autobiography, "Rosa Parks: My Story," written with Jim Haskins, details her life and role in the civil rights movement.

Despite her achievements, Parks noted in later years that she was not entirely happy, acknowledging the ongoing struggle against racism and discrimination. After her death, she was honored by lying in state in the U.S. Capitol, the first woman and only the second Black person to receive this distinction, recognizing her immense contribution to civil rights.

Biblical Example

Lydia(Acts 16:14-15)

"One of those listening was a woman from the city of Philippi named Lydia, a dealer in purple cloth. She was a worshiper of God. The Lord opened her heart to respond to Paul's message. When she and the members of her household were baptized, she invited us to her home. 'If you consider me a believer in the Lord,' she said, 'come and stay at my house.' And she persuaded us."—Acts 16:14-15

Lydia, as portrayed in Acts 16:14-15, holds a significant place in Christian history as the first convert to Christianity in Europe and a prominent businesswoman. Her story unfolds in the city of Philippi, a leading city of the district of Macedonia.

Lydia was a dealer in purple cloth, a luxury commodity in the ancient world. Purple dye was rare and expensive, often associated with royalty and wealth. Her trade in this high-value commodity indicates that she was a successful and possibly wealthy businesswoman.

This detail about her profession not only speaks to her economic status but also suggests a level of independence and influence uncommon for women of that era.

Her conversion to Christianity occurred when she encountered Paul and his companions. It is written that the Lord opened her heart to respond to Paul's message. This portrayal emphasizes divine intervention in her conversion, aligning her story with the theme of divine guidance and grace found throughout the Acts of the Apostles.

After her conversion, Lydia and her household were baptized, demonstrating her leadership and influence within her family or household. She then extended hospitality to Paul and his companions, insisting they stay at her home. This act of hospitality was more than just a kind gesture; it was a significant support for the early Christian missionaries. Her home possibly served as a meeting place for the early Christian community in Philippi, reflecting the role of house churches in the spread of early Christianity.

Lydia's story is representative of the important role women played in the early Christian church. Despite the patriarchal context of the time, women like Lydia were instrumental in the growth and sustenance of the Christian communities. They often provided crucial support through hospitality, financial assistance, and leadership within their local communities.

For many women, submission has felt like invisible handcuffs, holding them hostage and demanding obedience to male partners or leaders, even in hostile situations.

Photo Credit: **Rich Allela** and **Dapel Kureng**

Chapter 06
The Truth About Submission

If I then, your Lord and Teacher, have washed your feet, you also ought to wash one another's feet. For I have given you an example, that you should do as I have done to you. -John 13:14-15 (NKJV)

There is absolutely no way that we can address the truth of the Lady King's identity without paying homage to one of the most talked-about topics concerning the relationship between men and women—submission[12].

Submission is that word that most women dread to hear because its meaning has been misinterpreted, and misrepresented, and it is often the driving force behind much bondage for women. Considering the Lady King's revelation of equality between males and females, addressing this topic is essential—it is likely to come up in defense of male superiority. Thus, it needs to be addressed, and I am obliged to expound upon it.

The revelation of the Lady King marks the dawn of a new era for women, awakening God's intended purpose for His daughters. Through its message, women are encouraged to reclaim the mantle and the crown that

---

12 Submission: The condition of being submissive, humble, or compliant.; An act of submitting to the authority or control of another. —Merriam Webster Dictionary

was forfeited in the fall. Because we have entered this season of breakthrough and healing, now is as good a time as any to learn how to walk in our freedom.

> If God, being sovereign, granted mankind the freedom to choose, who are we to take away that freedom from each other? If submission is forced, Can we truly call it submission, or should it be labeled as control?

This newfound freedom requires us to challenge old systems of operation. Just as Matthew 9:16 states, we cannot pour new wine into an old wineskin. Attempting to do so would cause the wineskin to burst, and the wine would be ruined. Similarly, accepting women as Lady Kings will not work within old systems. We must challenge systems that have created subordinate norms between the male and female genders. In doing so, we may find that the world's definitions of specific terminology concerning women must be reevaluated.

We need to revisit old societal norms and cultural behaviors to determine if they align with this rediscovered truth of our identity. If not, they must be re-established, or we will have to reinterpret them. This task will not be easy, but I believe that God has granted us grace in this season to confront, tear down, and rebuild on a more solid foundation. Embedded in Kingdom truth, this new foundation will reveal the truth of women's position of power and authority and finally put to rest an ancient lie—that women are less than men.

For many women, submission has felt like invisible handcuffs, holding them hostage and demanding obedience to male partners or leaders, even in hostile situations. For example, a woman may remain in an abusive relationship with her husband because he traps her with the idea that she is obligated to submit, using scriptures such as 1 Peter 3:1, which states, "Wives submit to your husband.

I have even heard pastors say, "I will never tell a woman to leave her husband," often validating that stance with various scriptures and beliefs about how the woman should obey her husband. These types of convictions are based upon incorrect interpretations and systematic laws that have been intermingled with the Word of God. We must confront this pattern and demand that all of its practices cease.

It is precisely this type of barbaric behavior that we encounter whenever societal norms and systematic beliefs are accepted without measuring them against the Word of God. Carnally-minded individuals will produce their own laws and then create systems to sustain them. Whenever we accept those laws without measuring them against God's Word, we conform to a system that does not reflect God's plan for us. This may well be what the Apostle Paul was referring to when he advised not to be conformed to this world—meaning its systems of beliefs or its patterns—but to be transformed by the renewing of your mind.

> And be not conformed to this world: but be ye transformed by the renewing of your mind, that ye may prove what is that good, and acceptable, and perfect, will of God."—Romans 12:2 (KJV)

The renewing of the mind involves removing an old pattern of thinking and replacing it with a new one. This challenge was something Jesus encountered upon His arrival. So absorbed were the people in their own laws and legislations—even though they were incorrect—they obediently followed them. Jesus challenged these laws that did not align with Kingdom patterns.

> "Why do Your disciples transgress the tradition of the elders? For they do not wash their hands when they eat bread." He answered and said to them, "Why do you also transgress the commandment of God because of

your tradition? For God commanded, saying, 'Honor your father and your mother'; and, 'He who curses father or mother, let him be put to death.' But you say, 'Whoever says to his father or mother, "Whatever profit you might have received from me is a gift to God"'" — Matthew 15:2-5 (NKJV)

Jesus encouraged them to develop a mind like His—a mind focused on the Kingdom of God. Likewise, if we are to embrace the truth about our identity, we must cleanse our minds of worldly patterns that do not reflect Jesus.

I will admit that as I approached this chapter, I was uncertain about how to address submission without appearing to be against it. There have been many times when I questioned the hidden places of my heart, deliberately trying to assure myself that I was not walking in a rebellious spirit.

Like many women I know, I tried to accept what I was told regarding submission. And at times, I honestly believed that my thoughts about it were mistaken. This was because what I understood and believed about submission was dissimilar to what I had experienced. However, God began to reveal to me His heart on the matter. Consequently, I discovered that the world's definition of submission is somewhat different from God's definition.

To understand the difference, we must recognize the authority that humanity is given in the earth realm. That authority includes the right to make one's own decisions about a matter. Therefore, it is entirely possible that worldly definitions are crafted under the guidance of man's own heart. The problem with this is that man's heart is usually far removed from God's heart.

The Lord says, "These people come near to me with their mouths and honor me with their lips, but their hearts are far from me. Their worship of me is based on merely human rules they have been taught."

> *The Lord says: "These people come near to me with their mouth and honor me with their lips, but their hearts are far from me. Their worship of me is based merely on humanities rules that both create and taught to themselves." (Isaiah 29:13; NIV)*

For this reason, when we explore a topic such as submission, religion, or women's equality, it is imperative that we research the world's definition of them and then compare them to God's expressed will or desire for that subject. In doing so, we afford ourselves the opportunity to exercise our freedom of choice, which I believe always comes down to either choosing to follow Christ or not.

Moreover, a submission that is unmanipulated will present all the information about a matter—both pros and cons. It informs the person about the consequences that follow either choice. However, it is understood that the person has the right to choose either way. When submission is forced, it strips away the person's freedom to choose, leaving them with no other option than the one the perpetrator desires.

Submission Does Not Imply Inferiority

We are often taught that the person asked to submit is the weaker one, or that the person in authority or leading is not required to submit. For most of us, this approach sends an automatic trigger for us to rebel against submission on any level, especially for those women who are embracing the truth of their identity for the first time. It can feel strange coming into the awareness that you have been misled in this area. At times, you may even become angry as you learn of the hidden injustices toward women.

The stench of this inappropriate approach to submission seems to linger on long after we have discovered who we are, often carrying with it the penalty of unacceptance by male leaders and peers whenever rejected. The only way to remove its painful grips is to redefine its definition with a Godly one.

When you enslave something or someone, you place yourself in a position of superiority over them, thus demanding that they follow or obey you without question; this is not submission. Submission is a voluntary act. It is a decision agreed upon by both parties. Within the context of the decision, both individuals recognize the legal right of the other to choose not to submit.

Throughout scripture, there are no instances where God forces someone to act against their will or manipulate[13] situations to compel obedience to His commandments. Consider Deuteronomy 30:19-20; in these verses, God offers complete transparency. He presents the best solution to Israel, yet He does not demand its acceptance. Instead, He leaves the choice up to them. This demonstrates God's divine honor for His created humanity and the principle or law of free-will that He (God) gifted to humanity as a whole.

"I call heaven and earth as witnesses today against you, that I have set before you life and death, blessing and cursing; therefore choose life, that both you and your descendants may live; that you may love the Lord your God, that you may obey His voice, and that you may cling to Him, for He is your life and the length of your days; and that you may dwell in the land which the Lord swore to your fathers, to Abraham, Isaac, and Jacob,

[13] Manipulation: Manipulation is a noun that refers to the action of influencing or controlling someone or something to one's advantage, often in a way that is unfair or dishonest.

to give them." -Deuteronomy 30:19-20 (NKJV)

When God placed mankind in the Garden of Eden, He did not trick them into following Him. Instead, He presented them with the whole truth, making them aware of the consequences of their choices (Genesis 2:15-17).

Considering God's sovereignty and His decision to grant humanity the freedom to choose, it raises a critical question: Who are we to strip that freedom from one another? And if this freedom is taken away, can we genuinely label the resulting behavior as submission, or is it more accurately described as control or enslavement?

We must consider that God, who possesses sovereign authority, respects the legal right of His creations to make their own choices. By doing so, He welcomes a love that is willingly reciprocated by us, rooted in mutual respect and honor.

It may seem radical to some to believe that we can share mutual honor with our sovereign God. Yet, when we consider that He created us in His image, as His reflections, it becomes evident that God honors His creation. Consequently, if God extends honor to His daughters, isn't it reasonable to expect that we should receive the same level of honor from our male counterparts?

You are a King Not A Slave.

"Submitting to one another in the fear of God. Wives, submit to your own husbands, as to the Lord. For the husband is the head of the wife, as also Christ is the head of the church; and He is the Savior of the body. Therefore, just as the church is subject to Christ, so let us be to our own husbands in everything. Husbands, love your wives, just as Christ also loved the church and gave Himself for her, that He might sanctify and cleanse her with the washing of water by the word."

-Ephesians 5:21-26

God never wanted control; He desired beautiful submission. But not a submission obtained under tyrannical demands—God is not a bully. Any submission that is forced is not submission at all—it is control. As I stated earlier, to control something means to enslave it. God wasn't and isn't seeking slaves. Instead, He wants to lavish us with His love, a love that makes submitting easy.

> In this sacred space, love paves the way for vulnerability and sweet surrender. Thus, in its truest form, submission is a response to love."

Therefore, He endowed us with the freedom to choose. He then enveloped us in His love, revealing to us its depth, height, width, and breadth. He encourages us to willingly submit to this perfect love, a love that will never fail or cause harm.

Godly marriages should mirror this kind of submission. It should never be about one person ruling over the other. Rather, the love of God, flowing from the hearts of both partners, should create a sanctuary of safety. In this sacred space, love paves the way for vulnerability and sweet surrender. Thus, in its purest form, submission is a response to love."

"That He might present her to Himself a glorious church, not having spot or wrinkle or any such thing, but that she should be holy and without blemish. So husbands ought to love their own wives as their own bodies; he who loves his wife loves himself. For no one ever hated his own flesh but nourishes and cherishes it, just as the Lord does the church. For we are members of His body, of His flesh and of His bones. 'For this reason, a man shall leave his father and mother and be joined to his wife, and the two shall become one flesh.' This is a great mystery, but I speak concerning Christ and the church."

-Ephesians 5:21-32 (NKJV)

However, many wives have been enslaved by the misrepresentation of marital submission. And although it disturbs me to admit, the definition of the wife often dwindles to that of a cook, cleaning person, baby maker, do-girl, etc. Thus, making it hard for us to pinpoint a definitive definition of the Lady King's role as a wife.

Apostle Paul's concept of submission in Ephesians 5:21-23 reflects the submission between the Father and humanity. This type of submission is a mutual exchange of respect, where neither party is allowed to control the other. The dialogue in this passage is particularly intriguing as it appears to weave in and out in a cause-and-effect manner. Notice that Verse 21 starts with "submitting to one another out of reverence for Christ." This reverence is not akin to fear in terms of terror but rather a profound respect or submission to the will of God, establishing the foundation upon which marital submission should be based—submission to the Father first.

I submit that for the born-again Lady King, her submission to anybody or anything, including a spouse, must hinge on this foundational truth—is he submitted to Christ first?

After laying the foundation for submission between a husband and a wife, the Apostle goes on to say wives submit to your own husband as unto the Lord. There is that similarity again. As you would submit to the love of a good Father that is willing to lay down His life for you; so, shall you submit to this type of love that is found in your husband. It is this type of love that is worthy of the honor of submission. Not abuse, not control, and certainly not based on gender only.

Here is where freedom of choice comes into play. Whenever something is presented to you that is operating outside of God's prescribed method, you have the freedom, in fact, the God-given right to choose not to accept it. Thus, we must understand that submission to a spouse is not an entitlement. Instead, it is granted based on the condition of his heart toward God in any given situation.

We need only look to our Heavenly Father as an example of this truth. God has the power to wipe humanity out at any given time. He could force everyone to do what He says in a tyrannical manner. But He never strips us of our freedom of choice. Yet, this practice is found in marriages all over the world, and the idea of entitlement to submission for the male is preached even from the pulpit. This type of teaching has taught us to become slaves more than wives, leading us to give up visions and dreams and succumb to the fantasies of our husbands, all in the name of submission.

Our demand for equality has been acknowledged in some areas, yet the expectations placed on women have not fundamentally changed. We are merely allowed to operate in certain spheres, provided we continue to serve under the veil of inferiority to men. Women are expected to work nine-hour days, come home to cook, assist the children with homework, clean the house, do laundry, provide sexual pleasure to their husbands, and then get up the next day to repeat the cycle. When we voice our complaints, we are reminded that we asked for equal rights. We must ask ourselves—What is fair about this arrangement? And when will we see the part where the husband's love mirrors that of Christ's love for the church? Or when do we reach the point where the husband's submission kicks in, and we become partners rather than slave and master?

I must warn you that this inequity in marriage is deeply embedded in the minds of many people. To undo its stifling effects within marriages will require prayer, consistency, and confrontation. In the end, you will need to rise from the darkness reposition your crown, and remind yourself that you are king too!

You will need to resist the old patterns of submission to which you previously agreed. Additionally, you must accept that this level of change may be too much for some to grasp. Therefore, you should prepare your heart for those who may walk away. As you learn to exist within your newfound identity, your life will change for the better. And God will provide for you a company of Kings and Priests who will share your heart posture and welcome you in the full embodiment of your truth. (you are ezer-kenegdo—you are help!)

Submission Beyond Marriage

Therefore, you must be subject, not only because of wrath but also for conscience' sake. For because of this, you also pay taxes, for they are God's ministers attending continually to this very thing. Render, therefore, to all their due: taxes to whom taxes are due, customs to whom customs, fear to whom fear, honor to whom honor. -Romans 13:5-7 (NKJV)

Control exerts its hold in part by instilling fear. While we often associate control with physical restraint, it can also be enforced both mentally and physically. Misinterpretations of submission have led many women to submit unquestioningly to all forms of authority, including abusive ones. As a result, many of us find ourselves habitually yielding to everyone and everything, often driven by fears that have haunted us since childhood. The fear of rejection, abandonment, and both physical and verbal abuse becomes our burden if we dare to defy the world's expectations of submission.

"Before I move on, I want you to know something, Lady Kings—God hates an unjust weight (Proverbs 11:1). And He has taken notice of every tear that you have cried. He understands your brokenness. He was with you in your times of wandering as you shifted from one place to the next trying to find acceptance (Psalms 56:8). He wants you to know that you are not a castaway."

For a woman who hasn't fully grasped her own identity, any scenario in her life can make her susceptible to control by others, particularly in the workplace. Many women experience a sense of inferiority compared to their male colleagues, making it difficult for them to stand up or challenge them. Consequently, the true abilities and talents of countless women are underutilized in their professional roles. This underutilization is often a result of fear of rejection and a hope for validation from male figures—a validation that, for many, sadly may never come. As a result, these women often find themselves in a state of waiting, and so their dreams and visions remain unfulfilled.

We are now well into the year 2023, and the world still gasps in awe when a woman is elected to any office or if she is named CEO of a Fortune 500 company. Further proving that women have not come as far as we should have by now. If we truly accepted equality between males and females, a woman in authority would be a common thing. However, we have much work to do because not only do we need to advocate for society to view women and men as equal, but we must also lobby for women to change their perception of themselves. It is only when we can accept equality for ourselves that we will begin to embrace our freedom in Christ and refuse to accept or be a part of anything that opposes that freedom.

For most authoritarian leaders, their greatest fear is encountering a 'Lady King' who has fully embraced her true identity. Once she has acknowledged this truth, there is no going back to her previous way of thinking. Standing firm in her newfound self-awareness, she effectively dismantles any form of control exerted over her. She will radiate strength and courage, capable of engaging in healthy and constructive confrontation. No longer will she function as a subordinate or a silent participant; instead, she will emerge as a partner, a leader, a collaborative colleague, and an undeniable force.

The strange thing about most people's convictions on submission is that it seems sound, especially when advocated for with misinterpreted scripture. Also, those beliefs are usually laced with ignorance, arrogance, insecurity, and pride. And they are used to satisfy someone else's need to be validated. For that reason, fear seems to increase in men and women whenever the world's standard of submission is challenged.

Indeed, submission is not wrong, and for the Lady King who's healed, submission is an honorable thing, because she understands that submitting does not mean relinquishing her God-given authority.

Healthy Submission

It is high time for us to cast aside our 'slave clothes' and start embodying the woman God intended us to be. Yes, this transformation will likely lead to confrontation. To many, the confidence of a Lady King may appear arrogant or conceited, simply because the world is used to seeing her submissively bow her head, even in detrimental situations. However, this is the challenge we must face, my lady. By staying true to this course, we will gradually see our crowns return to their rightful place.

I believe the world is anticipating the emergence of the kings. Yet, many have yet to grasp that these kings also wear dresses. This very notion of a Lady King may be the most unsettling aspect for some. If that's the case, our mission is to champion a change in mindset across society. However, this advocacy for change must be carried out with grace and power and executed with humble hearts.

When someone has been held hostage or in captivity for a long time with no hope of freedom, the first news of liberty can cause an uproar. The awakening is usually very intense. When first awakened to the truth, the average person will often fight hysterically to prove that truth. That response rarely achieves the desired results, because it is often driven by partial insight and uncontrolled emotions. And the individual may adopt the mindset that he/she has the right to defy all authority.

As we grow in our understanding of our identity, our desire to embrace submission, as God intended, should deepen. This is a reflection of choosing to follow Christ and accepting kingdom principles. It's important to remember that being misguided in the past does not justify poor behavior.

It's crucial to recognize that the changes following our discovery of truth need to be embraced and shared with others in a spirit of love. We must be vigilant that this new awareness does not lead us to reject all forms of authority. In fact, it should guide us to recognize and uphold Godly authority while gently dismissing misguided authority, all done with love and understanding.

Therefore, we should not become barbaric like some of our male counterparts and begin to mistreat them. Instead, we must demonstrate Godly submission. We do that with class; we do it with boldness, and we do it with the assurance in our hearts that we will honor and respect others, but we will never again bow in submission as a slave does to ungodly behavior.

In doing so, some will rally you on. Others will despise and dismiss your efforts. But you, my lady, are strong. You are resilient; you are the force that the enemy is afraid to battle. Steady your course! Fix your crown and lead on! The fight is in your gracefulness, and the power that you possess is anchored in your identity. You are a Lady King. You are not inferior to the male. Submit to Kingdom principles and dismiss whatever is not. Do it with love, do it with peace, and when you do, never regret that you refused to be enslaved by injustice.

"May your heart remain anchored in God's truth. May you submit to His Kingdom and forever deny all else." -Selah

06: The Truth About Submission

Angela Davis (born 1944) | Activist and Philosopher

"You must never be fearful about what you are doing when it is right."— Angela Davis

Angela Davis, born on January 26, 1944, in Birmingham, Alabama, is a renowned American black activist, philosopher, and academic. She gained international prominence during her imprisonment and trial on conspiracy charges in 1970–72. The daughter of Alabama schoolteachers, Davis pursued her education both in the U.S. and abroad, eventually becoming a doctoral candidate at the University of California, San Diego, under Marxist professor Herbert Marcuse.

Despite her excellent record as an instructor at the university's Los Angeles campus, her political opinions led to the non-renewal of her appointment as a lecturer in philosophy by the California Board of Regents in 1970. However, she later became a professor in the field of the history of consciousness at the University of California, Santa Cruz, and was appointed a presidential chair in 1995, becoming professor emerita in 2008 .

In the 1960s and '70s, Davis was a staunch advocate for the rights of black prisoners and became particularly involved in the case of George Jackson, one of the Soledad Brothers. Her suspected complicity in a failed escape and kidnapping attempt led to her becoming one of the Federal Bureau of Investigation's most wanted criminals. She was arrested in New York City in October 1970 and faced charges of kidnapping, murder, and conspiracy, but was acquitted of all charges by an all-white jury.

Davis is also an accomplished author, having published several influential works. In 1974, she published "Angela Davis: An Autobiography," and she has written other significant books such as "Women, Race, & Class" (1981), "Women, Culture, and Politics" (1989), "Blues Legacies and Black Feminism: Gertrude 'Ma' Rainey, Bessie Smith, and Billie Holiday" (1998), and "Are Prisons Obsolete?" (2003). Her contributions to literature and social justice have been widely recognized and continue to inspire activists and scholars globally.[14]

---

[14] Britannica, T. Editors of Encyclopedia (2023, November 9). *Angela Davis. Encyclopedia Britannica*. https://www.britannica.com/biography/Angela-Davis
Copy Citation

The return of the crown for the Lady King will mean a return to her God-given identity in every area of her life. It is her wake-up call to re-posture herself in the earth realm and to reclaim the crown that was so viciously torn from her.

Photo Credit: Rich Allela and Dapel Kureng

Chapter 07

The Return of The Crown

For Zion's sake, I will not hold My peace, And for Jerusalem's sake, I will not rest, Until her righteousness goes forth as brightness, And her salvation as a lamp that burns. The Gentiles shall see your righteousness, And all kings your glory. You shall be called by a new name, Which the mouth of the Lord will name. You shall also be a crown of glory In the hand of the Lord, And a royal diadem In the hand of your God. –Isaiah 62:1-3 (NKJV)

Despite what many may think, our fight for equality and restoration of our identity far exceeds the need for a mere moment in the pulpit or to have our faces on the next ministry flyer. Instead, it is a fight to uncover and rediscover our true identity. It is the demand that the crown is returned to Her Majesty with every precious stone that accompanies it.

The return of the crown for the Lady King will mean a return to her God-given identity in every area of her life. It is her wake-up call to re-posture herself in the earthly realm and to reclaim the crown that was so viciously torn from her. It will require a realignment of the mind of the Man-King so that he may once again see the woman as a suitable helpmate.

It is a declaration to the nation that once she discovers who she is, she will never go silent again. It is a demand to the church to abolish its laws of inequity between males and females. And to come into agreement with the word of God, which states that in the latter days both His sons and daughters will prophesy. (Joel 2:28, Acts 2:17) Finally, it is a call to the marketplace to behold the Lady King in all of her Glory and to realize the depth of what she brings to any company.

The crown will not return hollowed out and empty. Instead, it will be returned with the precious stones of old. These stones will tell the story of our captivity and exemplify our kingship in every area of our lives. They will be reminders of the places in which we were once broken, but they will also testify to the redeeming power of God.

The Precious Stone of Redemption - Diamond:

Redemption: means; *to rescue, atone for guilt, deliverance from sin, or to repurchase.* -Merriam-Webster Dictionary

This gem represents the Lady King's redemption, shining as brilliantly as a diamond. Just as a diamond is precious and enduring, redemption is a priceless gift that brings lasting transformation. Like a diamond, redemption reflects light and beauty, showcasing the Lady King's renewed identity and purity.

The coming of Christ was God's way of reconciling the world back to Himself. Through our faith in Jesus, God nullified the effects of the sinful fall of mankind; thus, redeeming us from the burden of the curse. However, total redemption has often been forbidden for the Lady King. Not by God but by society in general.

In most Christian circles, redemption is the core of our messages. Many sermons are celebrations of our freedom from the curse of sin. Through these sermons, we have heard declarations such as God has redeemed the time and healed the land, even that our finances have been redeemed. But ironically when it comes to women, this redemption seems to be preached under the veil of exclusion. In the eyes of men, our redemption has been minimal at best: as women are forced to live under the curse with no hope of ever being free. For example, women can partake of salvation as it pertains to going to heaven. However, we are constantly reminded that we have no equality with men. If redemption has done its work and the entire world has been redeemed, it will place us back in a pre-fall position. In which man and woman were created equally and given the same command by God.

We can find substantial evidence of the woman's redemption in Luke 1:26-56. When the time had come for the savior of the world to be born, the first person restored was the woman.

The Angel appeared to Mary first, not Joseph. In lieu of this, we must consider that God is sovereign, and He knows everything. It was God who handed the curse down to both Eve and Adam. If the curse were never meant to be overturned, God would have been contradicting Himself when He did not consult with Joseph about Mary giving birth to Christ. We should accept this as proof that God restored the woman's position as an equal partner with the male. She demonstrated her authority and power in the earth to choose to obey without permission from a male figure.

Mary decided to obey Christ without asking Joseph. In Verse (38), Mary responded of her own free will, "Be it unto me." God restored the woman's privilege to make her own decisions.

Much like Eve, Mary now had the opportunity to make a choice again. We should accept this as proof that forced submission is not the will of God for His daughters. Rather His care and endless love for us should prompt us to follow His command with the assurance that we are fully backed by Him.

The Angel spoke a word from God to Mary and foretold of a future event.

God restored the woman's ability to hear clearly from Him. Therefore, her spiritual hearing has been redeemed. We should accept this as proof that it is not the will of God for His daughters to remain in a position of waiting until a male leader releases them.

The stone of redemption has been placed back in the crown; and although many may disagree, God is the final word for the redeemed Lady King. No longer are we castaways. The moment that Mary agreed with the desire of the Father, Christ's redemption went into effect. When He had completed the process of the cross, He declared "It is finished." In the end, it was Christ who announced that the work was complete. Also, it was He who gave dominion and power back to humanity; that power is released to both males and females.

Ladies, this redemption process must be accepted before you can be free. Doing so will detach you from the dark betrayal of the fall and realign you with the original intent of your Father according to Genesis 1:26-28

May you always be aware of the precious stone of redemption whenever you are confronted regarding your identity.

The Precious Stone of Dominion - Sapphire:

Dominion: *Territory under a government; region; country; district; governed; or within the limits of the authority of a prince or state; as the British dominion. -Merriam-Webster Dictionary.*

The sapphire symbolizes the Lady King's regained dominion and authority. Sapphire is known for its deep blue color, signifying the vastness of the Lady King's territory and the authority she holds. This gem's durability parallels the enduring authority of the Lady King, now able to rule her kingdom with strength and wisdom.

In many ways, Eve suffered the same fate as her contender Lucifer had in the past. Long before his encounter with her in the Garden through the serpent, he had already been cast down from his position. He knew that what he offered Eve would result in displacement. He had also revolted against the will of God and lost his position (Ezekiel 28:13-17).

Similarly, when Eve disobeyed God, her crown was stripped, and she lost her dominion (her governing authority to rule in the earthly realm) and became displaced in her kingdom (Earth). The effects were immediate as Adam began to assert authority over her, even deciding what to call Eve. Before this moment, he had only had the legal right to name the animals.

Since then, women have struggled with uncertainty about where they belong. We've been misplaced in our homes, marriages, employment, and churches, given makeshift territories that define our domain. Phrases like "a woman's place is in the kitchen," "a woman is a homemaker," or "a woman should be home with the children while the husband works" have only given us governmental authority in what society considers low-level positions. These are feeble attempts by the world to define the domain of the Lady King because in large part we have been deemed unfit for any real authority.

In most cases, the amount of freedom given to women even in these areas is subject to the wishes and desires of a man. For many, even decisions as small as preparing a meal are at the discretion of the husband. Ladies, this is not submission; this is slavery, and it is not the will of the Father for us.

For this reason, the second stone that will be replaced in the Lady King's crown is the precious stone of Dominion. Through Christ's redemption, women, once displaced, have been reassigned their dominion and deemed possessors of the Earth again.

For the redeemed woman, her decisions in any situation must align with the will of her heavenly Father. Under the banner of redemption, dominion must rise again for women.

The areas in which we are allowed to dominate will no longer be up for debate, whether in the home, marketplace, or church. Replacing dominion will restore our God-given right to rule in every area of our lives, bringing us back into direct alignment with Genesis 1:26, where God gives both males and females the command to govern the Earth and everything upon it.

Possessing dominion again will mean equal rights and shared responsibility for both man and woman in governing the Earth. However, I must warn you that this challenge will be substantial. Many will dispute your resolve to have the same rights as a male when it comes to dominion. Some will even try to persuade you that your dominion is not equal to that of a man by using misinterpreted scriptures. When this happens, check your crown, remember redemption, and lead on, my lady.

"The highest heavens belong to the LORD, but the earth he has given to mankind." -Psalms 115:16

The Precious Stone of Authority - Amethyst:

Amethyst embodies the Lady King's restored authority and power of speech. Its rich violet hue signifies the royal nature of her authority, a gift from the Divine. Just as amethyst's color is regal, so too is the Lady King's authority, allowing her to decree with wisdom and grace.

> "She considereth a field, and buyeth it: with the fruit of her hands, she planteth a vineyard. She girdeth her loins with strength, and strengtheneth her arms. She perceiveth that her merchandise is good: her candle goeth not out by night." -Proverbs 31:16-18

Perhaps one of the saddest things to behold is a King positioned in his kingdom without the authority to decree a matter and see it executed. Fallen kings lose authority over their territory and are no longer able to give orders or exercise their kingship. Such was the case with Eve, even though she was given authority, it was stripped from her after the fall. Therefore, the third stone that will be returned is the precious stone of authority. It will mean the return of our God-given right to speak (without permission), have an opinion, or cast a vision that will set nations free.

The return of authority gives us our voice back in every area of our lives; this is a critical asset for us. Far too long we have sat silently as our minds flooded with ideas and visions that could bring deliverance to the world. Yet afraid to move forward because we have been conditioned to wait on permission to do so.

Many marriages may not be as prosperous as they could be because women are not allowed to execute judgment, give an order, or merely state an opinion. Sadly, without this kingdom balance, many marriages are failing to live out the purpose that God has designed for them. Man and woman were meant to function together in authority. Stripping one or the other's ability to exercise that privilege impairs the marriage. In doing so, one person gets a voice, and the other one doesn't. Thus, leaving many gifts and talents hidden, and the Kingdom of God suffers significantly from this injustice.

This authority will awaken with the crowning of the Lady King. If the Man-King can embrace this awakening, the two will become a unit most fierce in the earthly realm. Together they will be able to possess every mountain of influence they are mandated to possess.

Ladies, take up authority again, speak your opinion, cast your visions, and give yourself permission to obey God. Remember the days of old when you were silenced because of your gender. Embrace this new place, and never go silent again unless God has so ordered.

The Precious Stone of Power - Ruby:

> "Behold, I give unto you power to tread on serpents and scorpions, and over all the power of the enemy: and nothing shall by any means hurt you." Luke 10:19

The ruby represents the Lady King's newfound power and ability to conquer. Its vibrant red color symbolizes strength, passion, and the Lady King's courage to overcome obstacles. Like a ruby's fiery brilliance, her power emanates, enabling her to tread on serpents and scorpions, overcoming all adversities.

Redemption, Dominion, and Authority will invoke power. The revelation of the Lady King can be summed up in this final insert into the crown—the precious stone of power. These components together will produce an explosion of power that will protrude into the earthly realm.

Before the fall, the woman was free and in perfect alignment with the will of her Father. She was able to consider a matter and decide if it was good or bad. She had dominion, authority, and power. However, after the fall, these components of her crown were lost. And without them, she could not produce Godly results no matter how hard she tried. Likewise, until we embrace every element of the crown, we will by no means be able to walk in power.

Dearest Lady Kings, dominion is possession. Authority is permission, but power is the result of authority. No man can give you power; it is the outcome of you coming into agreement with who you are. This truth of your identity is the true awakening taking place in this season.

I am convinced now more than ever that we are going to see greater initiatives from women than we have seen before. We will begin to create our own platforms and facilitate Kingdom gatherings on a grander scale. The closer you get to the discovery of your identity, the more excellent the move of God will be through you. When you have completely accepted it, you will stretch forth your hands to decree a matter, and before you are done speaking, it will already have come to pass.

God is going to use the Lady Kings mightily in this hour to overthrow the kingdom of darkness. The return of your power has stirred war in the heavenly realms. You will sense it before it happens. You will Hear it before it comes!

"Daughters of Zion may your hearts be ready for what you are about to see!"

-Selah.

Highlights of A Lady King

07: The Return of the Crown
|Susan B. Anthony| Crusader /Women Suffrage Movement (February 1820-March 1906)

"Cautious, careful people, always casting about to preserve their reputations... can never effect a reform."—Susan B. Anthony

Susan B. Anthony, born on February 15, 1820, in Adams, Massachusetts, and passing away on March 13, 1906, in Rochester, New York, was a pioneering crusader for the women's suffrage movement in the United States. Her leadership as president of the National Woman Suffrage Association from 1892 to 1900 significantly contributed to the eventual passage of the Nineteenth Amendment in 1920, granting women the right to vote.

Raised in a Quaker household, Anthony was instilled with a sense of independence and moral zeal from an early age. She began her career as a teacher before moving into social reform. Her involvement in the temperance movement led to her association with Elizabeth Cady Stanton, and together, they became key figures in the fight for women's suffrage. Anthony's refusal to be silenced in the face of societal opposition marked her as a determined and zealous advocate for women's rights.

Anthony's efforts extended beyond suffrage. She played a significant role in the American Anti-Slavery Society and the Women's National Loyal League during the Civil War. Her activism was not without personal cost; in 1872, she was famously arrested for voting, drawing national attention to the suffrage movement. Her relentless campaigning and organizational skills were instrumental in merging various suffrage groups into the National

American Woman Suffrage Association, where she continued to serve as a key leader.

Susan B. Anthony's life and work remain a testament to the power of steadfast commitment to social justice and equality. Her legacy is reflected not only in women's suffrage but in the broader fight for human rights.

Biblical Example

Phoeabe-Deacon | Romans 16:1-2

In the narrative tapestry of early Christian history, Phoebe emerges as a figure of profound significance, symbolizing the power and authority God has bestowed upon women. Recognized by the Apostle Paul in his epistle to the Romans, Phoebe's role as a deacon transcends mere titular recognition, embodying the active participation and leadership of women in the foundational years of Christianity.

Phoebe's designation as a deacon in the church of Cenchreae, as noted in Romans 16:1-2, is a pivotal acknowledgment of her role. The Greek term "diakonos" used by Paul signifies a ministry role, one that entails responsibilities crucial to the church's sustenance and growth. This title not only affirms Phoebe's dedication but also underscores the authority she held within the early Christian community.

The role of a deacon during Phoebe's time was multifaceted, Involving teaching, pastoral care, and administrative duties. As a woman in such a position, Phoebe shattered contemporary societal norms, illustrating the egalitarian ethos that Jesus Christ himself practiced and preached. Her role is a testament to the fact that in the eyes of God, the call to serve and lead in His ministry transcends gender-based limitations.

Phoebe's journey was not just a personal achievement; it was emblematic of the broader scope of women's roles in the early church. Her leadership role paved the way for future generations, challenging the patriarchal structures of her time and demonstrating that women were not only participants in the Christian narrative but also shapers and leaders of it.

Paul's exhortation to the Romans to receive Phoebe "in the Lord in a way worthy of his people" and to offer her any assistance she required speaks volumes about the respect and authority she held. It implies that Phoebe was likely entrusted with the crucial task of delivering Paul's letter to the Roman church, a role that required wisdom, courage, and theological understanding.

Phoebe stands as a beacon of the power and authority bestowed upon women by God. Her story is not just historical documentation; it is a continuing source of inspiration and empowerment for countless women in Christian ministry. She symbolizes the breaking of gender barriers and the inclusivity that is at the heart of the Christian faith.

Phoebe's role as a deacon serves as a powerful testament to the authority God grants to women in His ministry. Her story challenges the confines of traditional gender roles and serves as a divine affirmation of women's integral place in the leadership and propagation of the Christian faith. In honoring Phoebe, we recognize the dynamic power and authority that God has always intended for women, reaffirming their essential role in the narrative of Christianity.

As Lady Kings, we must believe that the redemptive act that took place on the cross also covered our fallen state. Though once cursed for our sins, we have been redeemed by His blood.

Photo Credit: **Rich Allela** and **Dapel Kureng**

Chapter 08

Wake Up Lady King

"And do this, understanding the present time: The hour has already come for you to wake up from your slumber, because our salvation is nearer now than when we first believed. The night is nearly over; the day is almost here. So let us put aside the deeds of darkness and put on the armor of light."—***Romans 13:11-12***

When something of great value has been lost, a strategic recovery effort must take place to regain it. Teams of individuals are often put in place, each with a specific task to assist in the recovery effort. Similarly, the recovery of the Lady Kings' crown is about to undergo a massive recovery effort, and God has deployed the help of many foot soldiers to return the crown.

We have witnessed monumental victories in times past. We can recall hundreds of women who have made significant contributions to society in favor of equality for women. Their impact on their respective eras serves as a testament to our true identity. Throughout history, they have left permanent footprints that are worth following.

For instance, Maya Angelou stood resilient and strong as a poet, touching the world with her words. Her legacy lives on to this day, providing reassurance to other young girls who may one day feel the urge to put pen to paper and become inspired to write. Maya gave us our voice through poetry

Oprah Winfrey dominated television for many years. Born in a small Mississippi town with the odds stacked against her for any hope of success, she overcame a double challenge first as a black person and as a woman in television. Yet, we watched in awe as her talk show transformed into a legacy of greatness. She gave us our voice in the media.

In 2007 and 2017, Senator Hillary Clinton ran for the presidency of the United States, and although she did not secure victory, her courage in undertaking the task inspired many Lady Kings to believe that our day was coming. Hillary gave us our voice in politics.

In the early 1990s, Dr. Juanita Bynum set the church ablaze as she took to male-dominated pulpits. She preached the Gospel with unprecedented transparency for a woman, challenging us to preach it all. Her proclamation that her struggles were meant for someone else's deliverance resonated with women worldwide as they experienced deliverance through her obedience to God's command. Juanita is among those who gave us our voice in the pulpit.

We will not halt our efforts here because all that has been taken or lost must be recovered. The curtains have fallen, and the Lady Kings are arising. I hear God saying for this season that we must bring the crown home at any cost.

To do so, we must recover every fragment of our identity and align each piece with the Word of God. We cannot profess to be Lady Kings in the pulpit only to become slaves when we return home. As Lady Kings, we must believe that the redemptive act that took place on the cross also covered our fallen state. Though once cursed for our sins, we have been redeemed by His blood.

Many have spoken about the redemption of women, and some have even written about them. Other well-intentioned men have negotiated on our behalf. However, a promise was made that just as women had orchestrated their own captivity, they would also give birth to their own deliverance. Thus, women are the ones who must give birth to their own freedom. No man can restore the Lady Kings' positions. We must grasp the truth of our identity and free ourselves. —*Who can find a virtuous woman? She finds herself! Lady Kings it's time to arise!*

This revelation may not be favorably received by many. Yet, the consistency of our movement toward total restoration will eventually take hold. Finally, the world will embrace the fullness of who God created us to be.

"May we prepare to gather all the pieces and place them back in their proper places."

Highlights of A Lady King

08 Wake up the Lady King

Betty Friedan (February 1921-February 2006)

Betty Friedan, born on February 4, 1921, in Peoria, Illinois, and passing away on February 4, 2006, in Washington, D.C., was a seminal figure in the American feminist movement. Best known for her groundbreaking book, "The Feminine Mystique" (1963), Friedan explored the underlying causes of frustration and dissatisfaction among women in traditional roles.

Graduating from Smith College in 1942 with a degree in psychology, she initially worked in various jobs before settling into life as a housewife and mother, while doing freelance work. Her experiences and a survey among her college classmates led her to conduct extensive studies on women's dissatisfaction with their lives, culminating in "The Feminine Mystique." This work is credited with sparking the second wave of feminism in the United States.

In 1966, Friedan co-founded the National Organization for Women (NOW), a civil rights group focused on achieving equality of opportunity for women. As president of NOW, she led campaigns to end sex-classified employment notices, pushed for greater representation of women in government, supported the establishment of child-care centers for working mothers, and advocated for legalized abortion among other reforms. NOW grew to become one of the largest and most effective organizations in the women's movement. Friedan was also instrumental in organizing the Women's Strike for

Equality in 1970 and played a leading role in the campaign for the Equal Rights Amendment. Additionally, she was a founding member of the National Women's Political Caucus in 1971.

Friedan's later works include "It Changed My Life: Writings on the Women's Movement" (1976), "The Second Stage" (1981), which assessed the status of the women's movement, and "The Fountain of Age" (1993), which addressed the psychology of old age and challenged societal views on aging. Her memoir, "Life So Far," was published in 2000. Friedan's writings and activism significantly contributed to the dialogue and progress of women's rights and feminism.

My dear sister, your perspective of yourself must change before you can recover your image. You must come out of agreement with false truths and begin to see the world through the eyes of a king.

Photo Credit: **Rich Allela** and **Dapel Kureng**

Chapter 09

Recovering the Pieces

Therefore say, Thus saith the Lord God; I will even gather you from the people, and assemble you out of the countries where ye have been scattered, and I will give you the land of Israel—Ezekiel 11:17 (KJV)

The return of the crown is merely the beginning of our complete recovery. It will empower us for the mission of recovering the broken pieces. However, the task of recovery will be much easier once we accept the crown and all the benefits that come with it. The crown will assist us in identifying the missing pieces. It will give us the power to recover them safely. Through the grace of God, each missing piece of our identity will be recovered. Once all the parts are restored, we will see greater kingdom movement in the earthly realm.

Recovering the Image of God

'So God created mankind in His own image, in the image of God He created them; male and female He created them.' - Genesis 1:27 (NIV)

The first piece of our identity that needs to be restored is our image. We must retrace our steps backward to recover this piece, a precious truth that can only be found in the heavenly realm. It was the presiding will of the Father when He announced to the heavenly host His plan to create mankind.

This truth is neatly tucked away inside the revelation of our inclusion and must be traced back to the expressed will of the Father for His daughters. And because the carnal mind cannot perceive that which is spiritual, we must visit the throne room often and retrieve these hidden treasures of our identity. The question now remains: Who is willing to ascend the mountain?

Once you set your mind to discover this truth and to teach it to others, you will encounter spiritual warfare like never before. Distractions will come, and discouragement may follow. Your peers may question your initiative, and at times, you may feel as if you are fighting an endless battle alone. All of this is because recovering your image will unlock the mystery of your strength and your ability to overthrow the kingdom of darkness.

My dear sister, your perspective of yourself must change before you can recover your image. You must come out of agreement with false truths and begin to see the world through the eyes of a king. You must stand tall, lifting your head high and bowing your face in the presence of your Father. You must read the scriptures through the eyes of a daughter who is accepted in the beloved. You must understand that you were not created in a distorted image, nor were you created to be subservient to the male gender.

Your Heavenly Father is a good Father. He did not create you as a slave to another. His love for you is deeper than that. However, He makes it clear that we can yield ourselves to other things and become slaves to them of our own free will.

"Do you not know that to whom you present yourselves, slaves, to obey, you are that one's slaves whom you obey, whether of sin leading to death or of obedience leading to righteousness?" - Romans 6:16 (NKJV)

Again, we stumble across your freedom of choice, a legal right that God will never take away from you. But be mindful, ladies, of where your choices lead. It was against God's desire for Eve to yield to the voice of the serpent, and as a result, she lost her image.

The true Lady King is confident in her Father. Her trust is in Him, and she looks to Him for all her answers. She submits only to what is submitted to Christ. And if for any reason she is required to submit to another, it will be at the discretion of her Father. Her true identity is intertwined with her relationship with Him. She is fully aware of the consequences of not following Him. As Lady Kings, we submit to whatever is submitted to our Father, and for that, we make no excuses.

"My sheep hear my voice, and I know them, and they follow me: And I give unto them eternal life; and they shall never perish, neither shall any man pluck them out of my hand." - John 10:27-28 (KJV)

Our image depends on our relationship with our Heavenly Father. We will never find it in things that adorn the outward appearance, like makeup, heels, or fancy clothing. These are mere adornments that make the outside look good and often offer a mask for what is hidden beneath the surface.

Instead, we must anchor our minds in the acceptance of who God created us to be. Once this truth is settled in your heart, you will have recovered this vital part of your identity. You are made in the image of God, in His likeness. You, my lady, are a king.

Recovering Order in the Home

"Her children arise up, and call her blessed; her husband also, and he praiseth her." - Proverbs 31:28 (KJV)

The restoration of honor in the household will unlink women from the stigma of being merely housemaids. Instead, the entire family will honor her. Recovering this vital piece of a woman's identity is crucial for the generations to come. Too often, a woman's strength and authority are stripped away within the confines of the home.

Fathers are often viewed as the sole authority within the household, and through this misconception, young boys are taught that they are a superior force, while young girls are taught that they are weak or incapable of wielding real power in the world. This mindset often follows them outside of the household, influencing their choice of mates and submission to them, even in violent conditions.

My dearest Lady Kings, your daughters are depending on you to recover this piece of your identity. The proverbial woman's entire household recognized her value. She was not just a cook or the person that Dad told what to do. Instead, she was called blessed and held high honor within the household. She was the one who sustained the family line. She was "momma"—a true Lady King.

To recover this piece, you must become astute among your children. Your presence must exude wisdom. My dear lady, you must refuse to be dishonored. It must be made clear that you are not your children's buddy or pal; you are their mother, the one God called to pour into them and prepare them to pour into their children. You should be distinguished among them, and they should openly declare their honor for you.

Lady Kings, if you are not being honored by your children, position yourself for the shift. Demand a change, and if they refuse, stand your ground in prayer and perseverance, refusing to give up until the change comes.

Recovering Honor in Marriage

"The heart of her husband doth safely trust in her so that he shall have no need of spoil. She will do him good and not evil all the days of her life." - Proverbs 31:11-12

Many marriages are struggling due to the husband dishonoring his wife. In many instances, men fail to see their wives beyond objects of control. For many, they were taught that women are the property of men and, therefore, demand benevolent honor without feeling the need to reciprocate.

Like a slave master who fears an uprising of his slaves, so do men who have not grasped the concept of an equal partnership. Mistreatment, abuse, and domestic violence often stem from fear, leading to volatile acts in an attempt to control the person that they fear will break free. Far too many women have had to tell this story. However, God has restored the desire within women to be honored and respected, even as they give respect.

For the married Lady King who is just embracing her identity, this may prove to be a challenge at times. If your husband is set in his ways, he may resist your new-found freedom every step of the way. The extent of freedom in this area that you choose to embrace will be at your discretion. However, if abuse is involved, the answer is clear—once you discover freedom, you can never return to slavery, and enduring abuse without retaliation only works on those with an enslaved mindset.

For the mature Lady King who is not in an abusive situation, you must learn to gently guide your husband through your newfound freedom, as his misconceptions of superiority have been deeply ingrained in his mind. Give him time to embrace the new, more self-confident you, and remember to extend to him the honor and respect that you desire as well.

For the single Lady Kings, as you walk in your redemption, you will attract a redeemed Man-King. He will be impressed by you and driven by your ability to help him birth his dreams and visions. Your journey with him can begin and continue well. However, you must remember to seek God's guidance first, prioritizing His will over your own.

Recovering Honor in the Church

"Charm is deceitful, and beauty is passing, but a woman who fears the Lord, she shall be praised." - Proverbs 31:30

It is no secret that women have often been mistreated within the institutional church. Yet, we cannot recover all the pieces of our identity without restoring this one. The institutional church is a powerful earthly tool for advancing the Kingdom, and the enemy uses prejudices within it to hinder his most formidable opponent.

For many of us, we have settled into the idea that the church is not a place of empowerment for women. However, the return of the crown has empowered us to reclaim territory in this area.

The church needs women: this is not a biased statement, but a factual one. The Kingdom of God was not meant to be advanced by males alone. It was God's intention for both genders to work in unison to multiply His kingdom on earth. However, Satan seeks to disrupt this unity by sowing confusion between the two.

Since the time of the fall, men and women have often worked against each other rather than with each other. This division hinders the advancement of God's Kingdom. Therefore, if we are going to reclaim the King's position and win the world for Christ, we must restore the Lady King to a position of power and authority within our local churches.

Lady Kings, we recover these pieces by stepping out of hiding. We refuse to accept a lesser role within any local assembly simply because we are women. We do this with humility and love, with confidence in who we are. If you find yourself in a place where you are not received, shake the dust off your feet and move on. Furthermore, God has called women to build ministries that embody healthy leadership and equality between males and females. Thus, in this season we will see women building ministries in greater capacity than before.

Recovering Honor in the Marketplace

"She makes linen garments and sells them, And supplies sashes for the merchants. Strength and honor are her clothing; She shall rejoice in time to come." - Proverbs 31:24-25

Finally, we must recover honor in the marketplace. Women are strong visionaries who can hear a vision and bring it into the earthly realm. Similar to the institutional church, women are often leaders in the marketplace, yet they may not always receive the credit they deserve.

For some reason, we tend to revert to traditional gender roles in this context, where men take center stage, and women remain in the background. However, the return of the crown will abolish this outdated mindset.

How do we restore this vital piece of our identity? We follow the example of the proverbial woman by no longer asking for permission to be great. (Proverbs 31) We demand recognition and credit for our work. We create businesses that promote equality between men and women.

We challenge the status quo, refusing to limit our gifts and talents without recognition, honor, and respect. We consider fields and purchase them. We make no apologies for being a Lady King in the marketplace, doing so with humility, love, and passion. We refuse to be anything less than what God has declared us to be.

When all the pieces are gathered, the Lady King will rise in full power and authority, and the Kingdom of God will experience a gathering like never before. Men and women will work side by side, casting a vision that will save entire families and create wealth to sustain future generations. Finally, we shall behold the glory of humanity as God created it—both male and female, side by side, bringing heaven to earth.

"Lady Kings, may you recover every part of your identity and walk in the fullness of what Christ has for you."

Highlights of A Lady King

09: Recovering the Pieces
Shirley Chisholm | United States Congressman

Shirley Chisholm, born on November 30, 1924, in Brooklyn, New York, and passing away on January 1, 2005, was a trailblazing figure in American politics and a champion for equality and justice. As the first African American woman elected to the United States Congress and the first woman and African American to seek the nomination for president from one of the two major political parties, she broke significant barriers and laid a foundation for future generations of leaders.

Chisholm's early life was marked by her immigrant parents' strong work ethic and emphasis on education. She graduated from Brooklyn College in 1946 and later earned a master's degree in elementary education from Columbia University. Her early career was dedicated to early childhood education, and she became an authority on issues related to child welfare and education.

Chisholm's foray into politics began in the 1960s when she served in the New York State Assembly from 1964 to 1968. Her legislative work, particularly in the areas of child welfare and education, demonstrated her commitment to addressing the needs of those marginalized in society. In 1968, she made history by becoming the first black woman elected to the United States Congress, representing New York's 12th Congressional District.

In Congress, Chisholm was a passionate advocate for minority education and employment opportunities, and she was known for her outspoken stance against the Vietnam War. One of her notable legislative achievements was the co-founding of the National Women's Political Caucus in 1971, which aimed to increase the number of women in all aspects of political life.

Shirley Chisholm's presidential campaign in 1972, under the slogan "Unbought and Unbossed," was groundbreaking. Although her bid for the Democratic Party's nomination was unsuccessful, it symbolized a significant moment in the political history of the United States, challenging both racial and gender barriers in leadership.

Throughout her life, Chisholm authored two books, "Unbought and Unbossed" (1970) and "The Good Fight" (1973), where she shared her experiences and perspectives on social justice and politics. Her legacy as a pioneer and a vocal advocate for the rights of women and minorities endures, inspiring generations of politicians and activists striving to make a difference in their communities and beyond.

Biblical Example

Junia-Woman Apostle | Romans 16:7

Junia, mentioned in the New Testament of the Bible, is a notable figure for her role in the early Christian church. Her mention, though brief, is significant and has been a subject of considerable scholarly interest and debate.

Biblical Reference: Junia is mentioned in Romans 16:7 by the Apostle Paul. The verse, in the New International Version (NIV), reads: "Greet Andronicus and Junia, my fellow Jews who have been in prison with me. They are outstanding among the apostles, and they were in Christ before I was."

Interpretation and Significance:

Apostolic Mention: The most significant aspect of Junia's mention is her being noted as "outstanding among the apostles." This has led many scholars to recognize her as an apostle, suggesting that she played a crucial role in the early spread of Christianity.

Debate Over Gender: There has been much debate over Junia's gender, primarily due to translations and interpretations of the original Greek text. While early Church Fathers referred to Junia as a woman, some later translations rendered the name as Junias, a male counterpart. However, the consensus among most modern scholars is that Junia was indeed a woman.

Imprisonment for Faith: Junia's imprisonment with Andronicus (likely her husband or relative) suggests that they were prominent and active members of the early church who faced persecution for their faith.

Precedence in Christ: That Junia and Andronicus were in Christ before Paul indicates they were early converts to Christianity, possibly having converted before Paul's own conversion around A.D. 33-36.

Theological Implications: Junia's mention has significant implications for understanding the role of women in the early church. Her recognition as an apostle challenges traditional views on the leadership roles women held in early Christian communities. It suggests that women could and did serve in significant and authoritative positions within the church.

Legacy: Junia's legacy in Christian history, while based on a brief biblical mention, has become a symbol of female leadership and participation in the early church. She serves as an example of how women have been integral to the Christian faith from its inception, contributing to its spread and establishment despite societal and cultural barriers.

In summary, Junia stands as a testament to the often underrepresented and undervalued role of women in religious history, particularly in the formative years of Christianity. Her mention in Romans highlights the diverse makeup of the early Christian community and challenges preconceived notions about gender roles in religious leadership.

"A new breed of ladies are emerging, wide awake in this hour. These Lady Kings are bold, their ears attuned to heaven. Indeed, the kings are truly coming."

Photo Credit: **Rich Allela** and **Dapel Kureng**

Chapter 10

The Collaboration of Lady Kings

And he gave some, apostles; and some, prophets; and some, evangelists; and some, pastors and teachers; For the perfecting of the saints, for the work of the ministry, for the edifying of the body of Christ: —Ephesians 4:11-15 (KJV)

God's heart yearns for His daughters to be restored in every aspect of their lives. Many women bear wounds deeper than most can fathom, enduring relentless battles against the enemy's assaults. Their legacies, often marred by pain from birth, embody the tragedy of Satan's enmity toward women. Some entered the world into broken families, suffering molestation by age five. Others inherited the curse of poverty, sometimes spanning twenty generations of violation by this wicked spirit. Many silently endure domestic abuse, both physical and verbal, with limited hope for freedom. The tales of violation by family members, exploitation by authority figures, and degradation by trusted mentors are all too common.

With all this to rise from, one may wonder how will the Lady Kings ever be free. How will we reclaim a position of royalty while bearing the stench of exclusion? The answer lies within the pages of this revelation. A new breed of ladies is emerging, wide awake at this hour. These Lady Kings are bold, their ears attuned to heaven. Indeed, the kings are truly coming.

I am personally witnessing the emergence of new ministries developed by women of various ages and ethnic groups.

There has been a noticeable shift in gender representation on mainstream platforms. Women are increasingly taking center stage, preaching, and teaching a more transparent gospel. They are determined to ensure that every individual who attends their gatherings experiences deliverance. These developments signify the resurgence of the Lady Kings' power.

This revelation isn't about diminishing men or claiming female superiority; it's a declaration of freedom for women, a freedom that rightfully belongs to both genders.

The fall into sin taught us how to behave as slaves, often pitting one woman against the other. But the redeemed Lady Kings are uniting, ready for a collaboration that will usher in a new era. These relationships will not be based on financial status or ministry favoritism; they will be divinely orchestrated by God.

As women embrace their freedom in ministry, at home, in marriage, and in the marketplace, they will reflect the image of God. Understanding their identity will align them with their earthly ministry assignments. They will no longer feel the need to compete; instead, they will recognize the value each brings to the Kingdom. In doing so, they will realize that no single woman possesses all the parts needed for the vast expansion of the Kingdom of God on the earth.

Some will be called to serve the fatherless and the motherless, others to create ministries for the homeless, drug addicts, and alcoholics, etc. Some will focus on the marketplace, while others will impact the institutional church.

These collaborations will be massive, with women sharing ideas across states without fear of someone stealing their ideas. In the past, the enemy divided us with competitiveness; now, the collaboration of true Lady Kings will break that competitive mindset thus enabling us to rise victoriously to overthrow the kingdom of darkness. Our hearts must be made ready to embrace this new movement—As we declare, I AM FREE! I AM MY SISTERS' FRIEND, WE ARE OUR FATHER'S DAUGHTERS!

Many women are just beginning to understand their newfound identity and are creating ministries that, while well-intentioned, may be ineffective on their own. What we need is a *mass collaboration* that brings together various women's ministries to form a united whole. This collaboration will fortify our walls and rebuild our gates, preventing the enemy from plundering us any longer.

As we reflect on the redeeming power of God that brought us out of darkness; We must remember, that other women need that same experience, but it won't happen through superficial or poorly coordinated efforts. The return of the crown will teach us to embrace each other, fostering unity among women everywhere. *New ministry collaborations will spring forth like fresh water in a desert. Through them, many will come to drink, be delivered, and set free.*

In closing, as we stand on the threshold of a new era, *the collaboration of Lady Kings* is not merely a vision but a divine mandate. It is a call to unity, a call to break free from the chains of division, and a call to fulfill the purpose for which God created us. Let us remember that the return of the crown is not about competition but about a collective rise to our rightful positions of authority and influence. Together, we will rewrite the narrative of women in ministry, in homes, in marriages, in the marketplace, and in the church. With unity as our foundation and love as our guiding principle, we will leave a legacy of transformation for generations to come.

Lady Kings Take this Revelation and Run with it you are free to rule again!

—SELAH.

Closing Prayer

Heavenly Father, we stand before You now, at Your feet, basking in Your presence. Through You, we have grown stronger than ever before. This journey has torn down many barriers and led us to freedom. The truth we've discovered is undeniable – it is our reality, always there, right before our eyes: we are Your masterpiece. I am grateful for this knowledge and pray that every woman can embrace this truth. You have not excluded us; You are a loving Father who cherishes Your daughters.

I pray for the women who have embarked on this journey, that they may find solace in knowing You haven't left us broken. Instead, You have mended us, lifted us from our falls, and restored our crowns. Let them know, Father, that You are not displeased with us. We are Your kings and priests on Earth, equal to our male counterparts.

I pray that husbands will once again view their wives as Adam saw Eve – as equal partners, formidable and powerful. May the suffering of women cease, Lord. Extend Your hand to countries where victory for women and girls has been scarce. Disrupt the enemy's plans and shine Your light of truth. I advocate for new laws and legislation that empower women. May the hearts of those in the institutional church be reformed, and the hidden injustices against women be exposed.

I pray that young girls recognize their worth and understand they are masterpieces crafted by Your hands. Lastly, Father, may this revelation spread far and wide, touching women across the globe. Let women everywhere embrace their Kingship, and may the world recognize that yes, we are Ladies, but we are Kings Too!!!

About The Author

Connie Dotson | A Visionary & Leader in Kingdom Advancement

Connie Dotson stands at the forefront of Voice of Truth Ministries as its visionary founder. Her ministry is a beacon of transformation, dedicated to the bold pursuit of advancing the Kingdom of God. With an unshakeable devotion to her calling, Apostle Connie has established influential platforms that significantly impact Kingdom work.

Empowering Women through 'My Circle My Life' Ministry

At the helm of 'My Circle My Life' Women's Ministry, Apostle Connie is a guiding light for countless women. Her ministry is a journey of healing and self-realization, where women are encouraged to embrace their true selves. Her passionate commitment to women's liberation and confidence is evident in the nurturing and transformative environment she fosters, promoting personal and spiritual growth.

Cultivating Disciples with Go Discipleship Training School

Expanding her influence, Apostle Connie has innovated with Go Discipleship Training School, an online platform that offers extensive resources for believers. This digital school is a testament to her commitment to equipping and empowering disciples for effective ministry, providing accessible and in-depth insights into faith and biblical understanding.

Innovating in Ministry with Creative Concepts

Through Creative Concepts for Ministry, Apostle Connie collaborates with Kingdom builders, offering unique strategies for ministry advancement. Her deep insights and creative prowess are instrumental in realizing God-ordained missions and pioneering concepts that align with Kingdom values. A Life Dedicated to Kingdom Restoration

Her ministry is a portrait of dedication to the Kingdom of God. She is passionately invested in empowering women, families, and the Church, envisioning a world where total restoration is achieved. In this critical time for the Kingdom, her life's work is devoted to this divine mission.

Building a Legacy for Future Generations

Beyond her immediate projects, Apostle Connie is actively involved in developing books, ministries, and curriculums. Her vision encompasses leaving a robust foundation for future generations to build upon, continuing the vital work of Kingdom advancement.

A Transformative Force in the Kingdom

Her life and ministry embody a deep commitment to the Kingdom's values and principles. Her creative approach and steadfast faith are sources of inspiration, motivating others to join the journey of spiritual transformation and restoration. She is a true force in the Kingdom-building journey, guided by an unwavering faith in God's redemptive power.

Contact Information

Email:creativeconcepts4ministrity@gmail.com

Web: www.creativeconceptsforministry.com

Other Publications

- Exploring the Kingdom of God
- Fundamentals of Discipleship
- Ministry Development
- My Circle My Life (Self-Image)
- I am My Father's Daughter
- Revelation of the Lady King Workbook

References

Merriam-Webster. (2023). Revelation. In the Merriam-Webster.com dictionary. Retrieved December 2023, from https://www.merriam-webster.com/dictionary/revelation

Wikipedia contributors. (2023). Revelation. In Wikipedia, The Free Encyclopedia. Retrieved December 2023, from https://en.wikipedia.org/wiki/Revelation

Wikipedia contributors. (2023, December 21). Harriet Beecher Stowe. In Wikipedia, The Free Encyclopedia. Retrieved from https://en.wikipedia.org/wiki/Harriet_Beecher_Stowe.

The Editors of Encyclopaedia Britannica. (2023, December 21). Harriet Beecher Stowe. In Encyclopaedia Britannica. Retrieved from https://www.britannica.com/biography/Harriet-Beecher-Stowe.

Nobel Prize Outreach. (2024). Malala Yousafzai – Biographical. Retrieved January 1, 2024, from https://www.nobelprize.org/prizes/peace/2014/yousafzai/biographical/

Encyclopaedia Britannica Editors. (2023, December 12). Melinda Gates. In *Encyclopædia Britannica*. Retrieved from https://www.britannica.com/biography/Melinda-GatesMichal, D. (2015). *Womens History*. Retrieved from Women's History. Org: https://www.womenshistory.org/education-resources/biographies/harriet-tubman

Our World in Data. (n.d.). *Gender ratio*. Retrieved 2024 January, from https://ourworldindata.org/gender-ratio

Made in the USA
Coppell, TX
17 March 2024